SHAKE THE EARTH

HER ELEMENTAL DRAGONS BOOK THREE

ELIZABETH BRIGGS

For all the friends who help us get through the tough times

1

KIRA

I'd traveled the four Realms on foot, on horse, and even on camel, but nothing compared to riding a dragon. I gripped Jasin's blood red scales to steady myself as he spread his wings and glided over the Air Realm, lifting us higher and higher. Slade's arms tightened around me while the wind whipped at my hair and exhilaration danced through my blood. I grinned and glanced over at Auric, whose golden body glinted under the sun as he flew alongside us. Reven sat on the other dragon's back, his pose deceptively relaxed, though he was always ready to leap into action. A sense of rightness filled me at being surrounded by my four mates as we embarked on the next part of our journey.

"We're about to enter the Earth Realm," Slade's deep voice rumbled at my ear. He was probably anxious to get back to the ground. Slade didn't like heights or anything that prevented him from keeping two feet in contact with the earth. He never complained, but I could tell he was uncomfortable from the tension in his body every time Jasin ascended.

"We should find somewhere to stop for the night," I said.

Slade scanned the area around us. "If I remember correctly, there is a small lake northwest of here."

"I'll find it," Jasin's dragon voice growled out.

Another benefit of traveling by dragon—it was fast. Over the last two days I'd watched the desert fade away to grasslands and plains and now to forests that grew denser with each passing minute. Below us I caught sight of the border crossing between the Air and Earth Realms, where the guards glanced up at the sight of us flying overhead, but didn't seem concerned. Most of the world didn't know yet that new Dragons were rising to overthrow the old ones, but soon they would. The time for hiding was over.

Within a few days we'd reach the Earth Temple, where I would bond with Slade, allowing him to turn into my Jade Dragon while unlocking my own earth magic at the same time. I'd already bonded with Jasin and Auric at the Fire and Air Temples respectively, and later I would bond with Reven at the Water Temple too. While Jasin and Auric had been eager to become my mates, Slade and Reven had been hesitant until recently. In the last few weeks they'd committed themselves to our destiny and had finally begun opening up to me, but I wasn't sure they'd ever love me like Auric and Jasin did. Slade and Reven both had secrets from their pasts that held them back, and I was still trying to break through their barriers. If we had more time, I might be able to do it, but we didn't have that luxury anymore.

My mates had been chosen by the four elemental gods of Fire, Air, Earth, and Water to replace the current Dragons that ruled the world—and those Dragons were not happy about it. At the Air Temple we'd fought their Golden Dragon, Isen, and Crimson Dragon, Sark, and now they knew who we were. We had to hurry to the next two temples before the Dragons could stop us, and they wouldn't let us succeed without a fight. They would do anything to prevent me from becoming the next Black Dragon and over-throwing the current one—my mother.

I'd recently learned that the Black Dragons were descended from the Spirit Goddess and were meant to protect the world for a short time, before their own daughters would take their place. However, the current Black Dragon, Nysa, had found a way to remain in power and had ruled for a thousand years without having a daughter...until now. Until *me*.

I still couldn't believe she was my mother. I'd lived in fear of the Black Dragon and her four mates all my life, especially after Sark killed the people I'd thought were my parents. Their deaths had haunted me for years, and the sight of fire had sent terror through me ever since. Now I could summon fire myself, but I still worried about losing control of it and destroying innocent lives.

How could the woman who spread fear and death

throughout the world be my mother? And if she was my mother, then who was my real father?

As we entered the Earth Realm the sun dipped lower into the clouds, casting the sky in purple and pink hues. My stomach rumbled, reminding me it had been many hours since we'd eaten. Jasin's clawed feet hit the ground smoothly, and his blood red tail swished back and forth as I slid off his back. I stretched my aching muscles, which had grown sore from sitting on his hard scales for hours. At least my magic would heal me quick enough—a useful gift from the Spirit Goddess.

Auric touched down seconds later, carrying both Reven and Brin, Auric's former fiancé and my newest friend. Despite the dangers we faced, she'd insisted on joining us on our quest, and I appreciated having another woman in our group. She was also an excellent fighter and had guided us through the desert of the Air Realm without any problems. I had no doubt she'd be a valuable member of the team, even if I did worry for her safety.

After we all dismounted and stretched, we began to unload the supplies and gear strapped to the two dragons' backs. Once we were done, Auric and Jasin shifted back to their human forms. They both staggered a little as their wings vanished and their scales were replaced by skin and hair. They were both doing really well considering they'd only just learned how to fly, but I felt their sudden exhaustion through the bond we shared. Jasin had a little more

4

experience being a dragon, but he'd had to practice flying for hours to get it right. Auric, on the other hand, had taken to flight immediately, as if he'd been born in the sky. But I sensed they needed rest and food or they wouldn't be able to keep up this fast pace much longer.

We'd landed in a small clearing on the edge of a lake, which was otherwise surrounded by thick, dense trees. The six of us went to work setting up the camp, the routine familiar after many days on the road together, although it had become a lot faster once we didn't have to hide our magic from Brin anymore. She'd learned the truth about us at the Air Temple when we'd fought the shades that had waited for us there, and she'd taken the news pretty well, all things considered.

As Jasin moved to light a campfire for us, he stumbled over a small rock. I'd never seen him move with anything other than confident grace, a remnant of his many years as a soldier in the Onyx Army. His warm brown eyes lacked their usual hint of mischief, and his auburn hair was messier than normal. He was still ridiculously attractive, the kind of man who turned heads every time he walked into a room, but the hours of flying had clearly taken their toll.

I touched his arm lightly. "Let me do this. You're exhausted."

"I'm fine. I just need something to eat." He shot fire from his fingertips into the pile of wood, then gave me a weary grin. "See? Nothing I can't handle."

I shook my head at his display and went to check on Auric. He was using his magic to clear away debris from around the lake so we'd have a place to sleep that night, but his tall frame was slumped with fatigue. Like Jasin, his golden hair was tousled from the wind, and his gray eyes seemed more unfocused than normal. Where Jasin looked like the good kind of trouble, Auric had the face of an elegant, handsome prince—probably because he was one. His father was king of the Air Realm and Auric was fifth in line for the throne, although he'd given up that life entirely when he'd become my mate.

"Tired?" I asked.

"A little," Auric said, with a thoughtful expression. "Our endurance is greatly increased as dragons, but we definitely feel the effects of flying all day once we return to our human forms."

"Rest," I said, rubbing his back slowly. "You and Jasin have done all the hard work so far today. We'll finish setting up camp and prepare some supper for us."

Auric leaned close and brushed a kiss across my lips. "I'd appreciate that. Thank you."

"Hey, where's my kiss?" Jasin asked with a grin that was impossible to resist.

I leaned close to give him a quick kiss, while Slade pointedly looked away and Reven rolled his eyes. A stab of guilt tore at me for favoring Auric and Jasin over the others, even if it wasn't intentional. I was still figuring out how to handle all of my mates and keep them happy, though I wasn't sure

I'd ever fully master that skill. With four men as my lovers there was bound to be some jealousy and awkwardness sometimes, no matter how hard I tried to prevent it. It didn't help that Slade and Reven kept pushing me away either. I had to find a way to get closer to them quickly—and I only had a few more days before we reached the temples.

2

KIRA

While Slade set up our tents, Reven moved to the edge of the lake and yanked fish out of the water with his magic. Brin and I unpacked some of the other food we still had, and I noticed we were running low on supplies. We'd have to stop at a village and restock in the next day or two. When Reven returned with some fish, I attempted to roast them over the fire, but Jasin huffed and insisted I was going to ruin supper and took over. It was hard to argue when his cooking was much better than mine, and everyone knew it.

We settled around the fire and began eating, all of us too hungry to do anything but shovel food in our mouths at first. I tried to savor this rare, calm moment among Brin and my mates, as I had a feeling they would become fewer and fewer as our journey continued.

"We should reach the Earth Temple in two more days,"

Auric said, when the eating slowed. The temple was inside a peak called Frostmount, high in the northern mountains, where it was so cold few dared to tread. Another reason we'd have to visit a village soon. We'd left Stormhaven, the capital of the Air Realm, with the gear to travel through the scorching hot desert, not the ice and snow.

"What's the chance that the other Dragons arrive there first?" Brin asked, as she set her bowl down in the grass. She was one of the most beautiful women I'd ever seen, with smooth golden skin, flowing black hair, and effortless grace. It would have been easy to hate her, especially since she'd once been Auric's fiancé, but she'd managed to win me over somehow.

"Pretty high," Reven said, from where he lazily leaned against a small tree. "They had a head start and can fly faster than Jasin and Auric can since they don't have any passengers."

Brin tilted her head to the side. "But they don't know which temple we're going to, do they?"

"No, they don't," Jasin said, as he wearily stretched his legs out in front of him. "My guess is that two Dragons will be waiting for us at each temple. They might have troops with them too. We'll have to be prepared for anything."

Slade scratched his beard with a frown. "We barely managed to escape two Dragons at the Air Temple. How will we make it into this temple if they're prepared to stop us?"

"Assuming the Earth Temple is still even there," Reven

added, bringing back memories of the ruined Air Temple we'd visited.

"We need allies," I said. It was something I'd been thinking about over the last few days while we'd been traveling, and I'd come to believe it would be the only way for us to defeat the Dragons. They were more powerful and experienced than we were, plus they had the entire military at their disposal. We'd also learned recently that they could control shades, malevolent spirits trapped between life and death that wanted nothing more than to steal life from others. For all we knew, the Dragons controlled the elementals too, though we didn't know that for sure. The six of us didn't stand a chance against all of that.

"Allies?" Brin asked, her dark eyebrows shooting up.

I nodded. "Now that the Dragons know who we are and where we're going, there's no hiding from them anymore. They'll do everything in their power to stop us, and we can't defeat them alone. We need help."

"Who would help us?" Auric asked, as he ran a tired hand through his golden hair. "Even my father would be hesitant to stand openly against the Dragons, as much as he would like to aid us."

"The Resistance," Jasin said. "They're the only people who have dared to oppose the Dragons."

Reven crossed his arms. "Except they do it from the shadows. Would they be willing to actually help us?"

"It can't hurt to ask, but how do we find them?" I turned toward Slade. "You were once part of the Resistance, and you helped those prisoners in the Fire Realm find a Resistance base. Do you know of one here in the Earth Realm?"

He hesitated, but shook his head. "No, the one I knew of was only temporary, and that was many years ago. I doubt they would still be in the same place."

"That's too bad." I sighed. "Can you tell us anything that might help?"

"There's not much to tell. I made them weapons for some time, but I gave up that life. I thought I was done with fighting and revolution and impossible wars." He scowled. "It seems the Gods had other plans for me."

I rested my hand on his knee. "If we can find them, do you think they'll help us?"

Slade's eyes were so dark they were almost black, as if he was lost in memories he didn't want to revisit. "I doubt it. They don't trust easily and they don't like to take unnecessary risks or expose their people in any way."

"Maybe once we show them who we are, they'll change their minds," Jasin said.

"They will," I said.

They had to—they were our only hope.

Once we finished supper, Auric and Jasin retired to their tents while Reven took first watch. I went to the lake to clean our utensils and bowls and then left them out to dry on a piece of wood. By the time I got back the camp was quiet, filled with only the sounds of crickets and the wind in the trees, and everyone else had gone to bed too. Jasin and

Auric weren't the only ones who were exhausted after our days of traveling.

I peeked inside their tent and found them both fast asleep only a few inches apart. The summer night was warm, and they both slept without their shirts, showing off their tanned, muscular chests. Desire rippled through me as I gazed at them, and I removed my traveling clothes and slipped into the gap between their bodies. Jasin's hand slid around me to cup my behind, while Auric's arm draped across my waist. I let out a soft, contented sigh as their warm skin pressed against mine, while my magic helped ease their fatigue to give them energy to fly again tomorrow.

When I awoke, it was still dark and the camp was quiet. I carefully extracted myself from my two mates, threw on a dress, and climbed out of the tent. I disappeared into the brush to relieve myself, and when I returned I saw Slade leaning against a tree, keeping watch over our camp. I'd originally planned to return to bed with Auric and Jasin, but after seeing Slade there I couldn't resist going to him. With the Earth Temple getting closer every day, I needed to spend as much time with him as I could.

I moved close and breathed in the fresh, clean scent of pine trees and moist soil. "It's good to be back in the Earth Realm, isn't it?"

"It is," Slade said, as he straightened up. He was the largest of my mates and his broad shoulders were as wide as the thick tree behind him. With his dark skin, trim beard, and strong frame he had a rugged attractiveness that always made me feel safe and protected. I longed to be wrapped up in those muscular arms again and to press my lips to his soft, full mouth. "It's only been a few months, but it seems like forever since I left my village."

"I know what you mean." The girl who had worked as a huntress in Stoneham seemed like a distant memory, even though I'd been her not long ago. I'd changed so much since leaving that small town, as had the rest of my mates. "I wish we had time to return to Stoneham and visit Tash. I wonder if she's gotten my letter by now?"

"Probably," Slade said.

Tash had been my best friend for the last three years while I lived in the Earth Realm, but I'd left her behind when I'd embarked on this journey with my mates. I'd promised to visit if I could, but with the Dragons on our tail it wasn't prudent or safe. I'd sent her a letter from Auric's palace and he'd promised to use his faster courier, but there was no way to tell if she'd received it by now.

I leaned against the tree beside Slade and gazed at his serious face. "I would like to visit your village and meet your family too. Maybe once this is all over..."

His shoulders tensed. "Maybe."

My heart sank at his reaction, and I began to turn away. "If you don't want me to meet them, I understand. I know you didn't want this life."

His large hands settled on my waist, pulling me back to him. "It's not that. I'd like you to meet them, but I worry they won't have an easy time accepting this situation."

"You mean with the other men?" Multiple partners were almost unheard of in the Earth Realm, even though the practice was common in the Air and Water Realms. Slade had already made it clear he wasn't interested in sharing me with the other men. Sometimes I thought he might be able to love me if it was just the two of us in a relationship, but that wasn't an option. I understood his hesitation and respected his feelings, especially since this was all unexpected and new for me too. I'd never imagined I'd end up with four men, nor that I'd be able to have strong feelings for each of them, but here we were.

I would do whatever I could to make this situation more bearable for Slade, and the fact that he was still here showed he was willing to try to make this work. He'd originally claimed he was only with me because of duty, but when he'd kissed me it had felt like a lot more. And oh, how I longed for another of those kisses now.

His hands lingered on my waist. "The people in my village are very religious, but also very traditional. I'm not sure how they'll react to our relationship. It's a great honor to be chosen by the Gods as one of your mates, but sharing a woman simply isn't done in the Earth Realm. I'm still trying to accept it myself."

I slid my fingers along his bearded jaw, unable to resist touching him when he was this close. "I know, and I appreciate it. I wish there was something I could do to make it easier on you."

He took my palm and kissed it softly, and his tenderness

14

made my heart skip a beat. "It's not only because of the other guys. There's something I need to tell you about my past too."

"What is it?" I asked, leaning forward. I was greedy for any scrap of information about him. Anything to get closer to him.

He opened his mouth, but then froze as we both heard a rustle in the leaves near us. I reached for my bow instinctively, but I'd left it in Auric and Jasin's tent along with my sword. Slade unsheathed his axe and changed his stance, instantly ready to defend me from any threat. I moved into position beside Slade, summoning small balls of fire into my palms. I was unarmed, but I wasn't defenseless.

As we stood perfectly still, I caught the faint snap of a twig in the brush. We weren't alone.

3

KIRA

Men and women with scarves over their mouths and dark hoods over their faces slipped through the woods and surrounded us. I couldn't tell how many there were, but I estimated at least six from the quick glimpses between the leaves and the soft sounds of their movements through the brush. Bandits, most likely.

Slade let out a low warning growl, but the bandits didn't attack. That wasn't like them—from my time as a bandit, I knew they preferred to take people by surprise. What were they doing?

A hooded man emerged in front of me, and I prepared to strike him down with a lash of flame until I saw his sword was still sheathed. He reached up and slowly lowered his hood, and my eyes widened as I took in his familiar face.

"Cadock?" I asked, as the fire in my palms vanished.

"Kira," he said softly. "It really is you."

I nodded, speechless at the sight of someone from my past I thought I'd left behind forever. Cadock strode toward me with a smile, his blue eyes flashing under the moonlight. He was just as attractive as I remembered him, although his thick blond hair had grown longer since I'd seen him and now hung about his shoulders. His frame had filled out too, becoming a warrior's body instead of a lanky teenage boy's.

He threw his arms around me and drew me in for a hug. "Gods, it's good to see you. It's been far too long."

Cadock's embrace had once meant everything to me, along with his approval, but I was no longer that young girl on the run, looking for a new family, searching for someone to love me. I had my mates now and a new purpose.

I stepped back, but offered him a warm smile. "Four years."

"When one of my scouts said they'd spotted you by the lake, I didn't believe it, yet here you are." He brushed his thumb across my chin as he gazed into my eyes. "And somehow you've gotten even more beautiful."

Slade shoved Cadock's shoulder, pushing him back. "Get away from her."

"It's okay," I quickly told Slade. "He's a...friend."

Cadock arched an eyebrow. "We were definitely more than that once."

I gave him a sharp look. Did the man have a death wish? I needed to quickly change the subject before Slade ripped off his head. "What are you doing in the Earth Realm?"

Cadock gestured around us. "The Air Realm has

stepped up its patrols. We moved here a year ago and now wait for travelers on this side of the border. This is a good spot since people always camp by the lake." He gave us a wry grin. "Easy pickings."

"And you planned to do the same to us," Reven's voice said from the shadows. I hadn't even realized he was there.

Cadock shrugged. "We do what we have to do to survive these hard times. Kira did the same once."

"What is he talking about?" Slade asked, his green eyes narrowing.

"Ah, did she not tell you about that?" Cadock chuckled softly. "Don't worry, she gave up this life to settle down in a quiet town somewhere. Or so she said."

"I did, but the quiet didn't last," I muttered.

His eyes danced with amusement. "Of course not. You're not meant for a quiet life."

Jasin and Auric suddenly emerged from the tent, gripping their weapons and wearing only their breeches. Jasin asked, "What's going on out here?" while Auric called out, "Is everything all right?"

"We're fine," I said, raising my hands in a calming gesture. "I know these people."

"They look like bandits," Auric said as he lowered his sword.

Cadock let out a hearty laugh. "That's because we *are* bandits."

"Kira, I think it's time you explained," Slade said.

I sighed. I'd hoped I could keep this dark part of my past

a secret, but there was no hiding it now. I turned to face my men and met each of their eyes in turn while I spoke. "I was once part of Cadock's gang. I'll explain everything later, I promise. But right now I'd like to talk to Cadock alone. Please."

"Definitely not," Slade said, stepping closer until he was right against my back.

I pinched the bridge of my nose, then asked Cadock, "Would you give us a moment?"

He shrugged, with a hint of amusement on his lips. "Certainly. I'm curious to see how this plays out."

He and his bandits slipped back into the forest, and I gestured for my men to join me by the fire. Not a single one of them looked happy, though I wasn't sure if it was from the revelation that I used to be a bandit or because I wanted to speak to Cadock alone. They were overprotective at the best of times, even though I was supposed to be the most powerful of us all—or would be someday.

"Is it true?" Auric asked, once they were all crowding around me. "You were once a bandit?"

"Yes, I was." I drew in a deep breath to steady myself and continued. "I was fifteen when they saved my life from two men who tried to capture me, and I became one of them because I had nowhere else to go. That gang, the Thunder Chasers, was like my family for two years, and Cadock's father led us. Cadock became my closest friend, and he taught me how to use a bow and to live in the wild. But after his father was killed, things fell apart and the gang became desperate. I decided I wasn't comfortable with what they were doing, and I left." I paused, and then added, "I'm not proud of the things I did with them, but it's the only way I stayed alive when I was younger."

"Cadock implied the two of you were...together," Reven said, arching an eyebrow.

My cheeks heated. Of course they would focus on that part. "We were, yes, but we were both a lot younger then. Nothing happened except for a few kisses, and I no longer feel anything for him."

Jasin sheathed his sword but kept his hand on the hilt. "Good, but there's no way you're talking to him alone."

"Agreed," Slade said, crossing his arms. "I don't like this at all."

"Cadock would never hurt me, and even though he may look like an ordinary bandit, he's clever and has a lot of connections," I said. "If anyone can tell us where the Resistance is, it's him. But I doubt he will do that if I have all of you hovering around me and glaring at him. I simply need a few minutes alone, and we won't be far. Just trust me."

"I do trust you," Slade said. "I don't trust *him.*"

I sighed. "If he tries to harm me, you can toss a boulder on him."

"Believe me, I will."

Auric rubbed his chin as he considered. "If you think he might have some information that could help us, then you should speak with him. Just be careful."

"Thank you," I said, relieved that at least one of my mates was on my side.

"Fine, but one of us is coming with you," Jasin said. "You knew this Cadock guy years ago, but you don't know what he's like now."

Reven stepped forward. "I'll go. He'll never know I'm there."

"Fine." I wanted to argue, but knew it was useless. This was the best compromise I would get from my domineering mates.

I grabbed my sword and my bow, just in case, and then headed into the woods with Reven falling into step at my side. He moved with the easy, predatory grace that came from a life as an assassin, and I managed to get one last look at his dark, deadly beauty before he slipped into the shadows. With his raven black hair, ice blue eyes, and sculpted face, he was the most striking of my mates. Being near him always made my heart race, and while I should have been afraid of him, I'd always known he would never hurt me. Instead, a calm steadiness settled over me as I walked through the woods, knowing his keen eyes were watching over me.

I squared my shoulders and set off to meet the bandit I'd once loved.

4

KIRA

I found Cadock near the lake, waiting alone. His face split into an easy grin at the sight of me. "So glad you decided to join me for a chat. I thought your companions would never leave you alone."

I hoped I wasn't making a mistake by trusting Cadock. Though I didn't think he or his people would harm me, it had been a few years since I'd seen them and things had obviously changed quite a bit. My hand was ready near my sword, though I tried to look relaxed. "It wasn't easy to convince them you wouldn't escape with me in the night, but I managed."

Cadock laughed. "If you run off with me, it will be of your own free will, I promise."

I moved to the edge of the black water, which reflected the stars back up at the sky. "How have you been?"

"Busy," he said. "Things were hard after my father

passed, and only got worse over the years as the Onyx Army increased its patrols and food became harder to come by in all the Realms. I realized to survive we had to change our ways and join together with other gangs to become more than simple bandits. I convinced others to merge with us and we formed a sort of tribe. We now have camps across the four Realms and more people joining us every month."

"Impressive," I said. Cadock had truly stepped up as a leader over the years. "Your father would be proud."

"I hope so. But what are you doing on the road? And who are your companions?" He stepped closer, lowering his voice. "Has one of them replaced me as your man?"

"It's...complicated." I avoided meeting his eyes and then added, "I'm actually in a relationship with all four of them."

Cadock let out a deep belly laugh. "All four? Gods, you really have changed. Who would have thought little prudish Kira would take four lovers?"

"Just because I wouldn't sleep with you didn't make me prudish." I'd cared a lot for Cadock and had been tempted many times by him. We'd gotten close, but I'd always held back. Maybe a part of me had always known, deep down, that he wasn't the one for me and that I should wait for the right man—or in my case, *men*—to come into my life. When I'd slept with Jasin and Auric I hadn't felt any of that hesitation, it had simply been right, as if we were destined to be together. I'd never had that with Cadock, no matter how fond I'd been of him, or how much I'd desired his body. He might have been my first love, but he'd never truly had my heart.

"I apologize," Cadock said, holding up his hands in surrender. "It's simply hard for me to believe."

I had to confess the rest if I wanted to ask for his help, but it never got easier to say the words out loud. Especially to someone like him. "There's a reason for it. I'm the next Black Dragon."

Cadock scratched his chin. "I'm afraid I don't follow."

"The Gods chose us to overthrow the current Dragons and take their place. That's why we're traveling across the Realms."

He crossed his arms and gave me a skeptical look. "If this is some sort of con, it's the strangest one I've heard."

"It's not a con," I said, trying not to let my exasperation show. This happened every time I told someone who I was. I knew the blame was with the current Black Dragon for hiding the truth and spreading misinformation, and I'd once been just as skeptical, but sometimes it felt tedious having to convince people again and again.

"Then it's a dangerous delusion." Cadock shook his head. "I don't know what you're thinking, but you're going to get yourself killed if you go around talking like that."

Enough of this. I conjured a large flame in my hand, and he let out a short gasp. "I know it's hard to believe, but I am the next Black Dragon, and the others are my mates."

Cadock took a step back at the sight of the fire. "I caught a glimpse of you holding fire earlier but I thought it was sleight of hand or a trick of the light. It can't be possible..."

"It's real." I let the flames burn brighter as they danced across my fingertips. "We're going to overthrow the Dragons or die trying, and we're on our way to the Earth Temple now. But we need allies."

His eyes widened. "Allies? To fight the Dragons? No one is that suicidal."

Frustration settled over me as I closed my hand around the flame and let it die out. "I suppose that means you won't be joining our cause."

He let out a sharp laugh. "We're bandits, not soldiers. We don't fight for causes. We fight for survival and for riches."

"But you just said you wanted to be more than bandits, and we could use strong fighters who know how to survive in the wild."

"Maybe what you're saying is true, but what's in it for us?"

"The chance to live free of tyranny and oppression. Is that not enough?"

Cadock shrugged. "So we exchange one ruler for another. What difference does that make? We live outside the law anyway."

"But what if you didn't have to?" I asked, taking a step toward him and softening my voice. "I know you, Cadock. You're a good man with honor. We could offer your people a life where they won't have to run or hide anymore."

He reached up to touch a piece of my red hair. "I'm sorry, Kira. I still care for you a lot, but I have to think about my people, and I can't lead them into an unbeatable war."

"I understand." I bowed my head. Getting Cadock's help had been unlikely all along, but I'd still hoped I could convince him, especially once I'd learned how he'd changed over the years. As disappointing as it was, I couldn't blame him for wanting to keep his people safe, even if the fate of the world was at stake. "Perhaps you could help me with some information instead."

"Now that I can probably do. What kind of information?"

"We're looking for the Resistance."

He smirked. "Of course. The only fools who might be willing to fight by your side. Lucky for you, I know where their main base is located. Bring me a map and I'll mark it for you."

"Thank you," I said. "I really appreciate it, and we can pay you for the information."

He waved his hand. "No need. Consider this a favor for an old...friend."

We walked back into camp, where the others waited with suspicious eyes and tense shoulders. Auric brought out our worn, crinkled map and Cadock marked a spot at the edge of the mountains in the north, not far from the Earth Temple, and told us to look for a boulder shaped like 'two perky tits'—his words, not mine. As I scanned the map I noticed my old village Stoneham was directly on the path to it. Perhaps we'd have time to stop there, at least for a short while. We did need supplies, after all.

When Cadock was finished, I walked him to the edge of our camp and prepared to say our goodbyes. His eyes lingered on me with something like longing or regret, and he reached out to touch me again before stopping himself. "Kira, if you ever feel like giving up this mad quest, you're always welcome by my side."

A month ago his offer might have tempted me, but now I could shake my head with certainty. "Thank you, but this is my path."

5

SLADE

While the others packed up their things I stood under the trees near the lake, needing some space. It was the morning after our encounter with the bandits, and we were about to head out. I checked the map again, noting the supposed location of the Resistance base, and frowned. I'd never heard of a base there, but it had been years since I'd been a part of that world. Still, I didn't like it. We were trusting a bandit who likely would have tried to slit our throats and steal our things if he hadn't recognized Kira. Who was to say he wasn't sending us to our deaths?

"Almost ready to go?" Kira asked, as she moved to my side. Being so near her instantly made my body awaken in a primal way, reminding me of all the ways that I was male and she was female. Her shining red hair was tied back today, and a memory of brushing those long strands came to me, along with a desire to see her hair down about her naked shoulders, preferably spread out on a pillow below me.

"Just about." I shook off the thought and folded up the map. Jasin and Auric had shifted into their dragon forms and were stretching their wings and preparing for a long flight, while Brin and Reven were loading our supplies onto their backs. I couldn't believe they were all going along with this madness too.

Kira gave me a smile that brought back indecent thoughts again. Gods, she was beautiful. "We're going to stop at my old village to get supplies and rest for the night. We should make it to the base tomorrow."

I scowled. "Assuming there really is a base there. For all we know your 'friend' is leading us into some kind of trap."

"Why would he lead us into a trap?"

"I don't know. But I don't have any reason to trust a bandit either." Maybe he'd do it to make it easier to kill us and rob our corpses. Or maybe he'd do it to steal Kira away from us. Or maybe he just wanted to mess with our heads. How should I know?

She rested her hand on my arm and some of my tension faded. "You trust me though."

"Of course I do. But were you ever going to tell us you were a bandit?"

Her face fell. "I was going to tell you eventually. It's not exactly something you bring up in everyday conversation, and I was worried what you all might think." She looked up at me with hazel eyes that were tinged with worry. "Do you judge me harshly for what I've done?"

I sighed and pulled her into my arms, holding her close to my chest. The revelation about her being a bandit had come as a shock, even though I understood why she'd done it. I just didn't like the thought that she was hiding things from us. "No, we've all done some things we regret. I simply would have liked to know about your past before it came back and surrounded us with weapons."

Her fingers gripped my shirt as she gazed up at me. "I understand, but I'm not the only one whose past is haunting us. You mentioned there was something you needed to tell me, and you haven't explained how you got involved with the Resistance, but I'm not going to push you. We all have things we'd rather not talk about."

She was right, it wasn't fair of me to judge her for keeping secrets when I'd kept a few of my own. Secrets that would soon be uncovered once we arrived at the Resistance base. Better to reveal them now, no matter how much I hated talking about this part of my past.

"I'm ready to tell you now." I took a deep breath, and then I released her and stepped back. "I mentioned before that when I was younger I was close to a girl in my village."

"Yes, I remember."

I swallowed hard. Once the past came out, it couldn't be ignored or forgotten or avoided any longer. I'd have to finally face it. "Her name was Faya and we grew up together.

There weren't a lot of other people our age in the village and it seemed inevitable we'd be married. But that never happened."

"Thank the Gods," Kira said with a tight smile. "Otherwise you wouldn't be my mate."

"Indeed." I rubbed the back of my neck, trying to figure out the best way to tell this story. "Faya had a strong rebellious spirit and wanted change and progress. When she was a child her father was killed by the Crimson Dragon for speaking out against the tax hike, and that moment clouded everything she did, as I'm sure you can understand. She tried to fix all the problems in our village and as she grew older she wanted to fight against injustice. I was the one who balanced her out and steadied her, especially when her passion made her act without thinking. But eventually I wasn't enough."

"What happened?" Kira asked.

"Faya became involved with the Resistance, who had a small camp near our village, and it was like she'd finally found her true calling. She encouraged me to get involved too, but I was hesitant because of the danger involved. I agreed to make them weapons and armor, but no more, and only because I loved her and could tell this was important to her. We were engaged to be married by that time, and I suppose I thought she would settle down once we were wed." I shook my head, disgusted at my younger self. "I was a fool. She began to spend more and more time with the

Resistance, and especially their leader, Parin. I grew jealous and worried about her safety, and we fought a lot. She planned to become more active in the fight against the Dragons, and I longed for a quiet life without trouble. I wanted to be a husband, a father, and a blacksmith. She wanted to be a revolutionary." I turned away from Kira, unable to look at the pity in her eyes as I got out this next part. "On the eve of our wedding, Faya confessed she'd been sleeping with Parin and had fallen in love with him. She wanted to join the Resistance permanently and she asked me to come too. She said she still loved me and wanted to be with both of us. Parin had already agreed to share her...but I couldn't do it."

"Oh, Slade, I'm so sorry." Kira slid her arms around me from behind, resting her head on my back.

"After that night, I cancelled our wedding and cut all ties with the Resistance. I never saw her again." I turned toward Kira and returned her embrace, cradling her in my arms. "But that was many years ago. I've moved on with my life, and I see now that it was all for the best. I wasn't blameless either—I never should have tried to tame her spirit or prevent her from doing what she felt was right. And if I had stayed with her, I wouldn't be with you now."

Her brow wrinkled. "Are you sure you're happy with that? We'll likely never have a quiet life. Being with me goes against everything you wanted before."

"What I want has changed over the last few weeks with you." I pressed a kiss to her forehead. "I simply wanted you to know about Faya before we arrived at the Resistance base, as there might be some...awkwardness if she and Parin are there."

"Thank you for telling me." She rested her head against my shoulder. "That must have been horrible for you. She cheated on you and betrayed your trust. No wonder you've been so resistant to this relationship."

I stroked her hair as I held her close. "This path the Gods have sent us on has been unexpected and difficult to accept sometimes, but I'm committed to you and to our duty. Never doubt that."

"I know." Her eyes fixed on the collar of my shirt, and her voice came out hesitant. "Although I hope you'll come to care for me as well."

"I already do." Now that I'd revealed my past, speaking the words came easier. I slid my hand along the soft skin of her face, before tangling my fingers in the hair at the base of her neck. "Kira, I've always cared for you."

Her eyes flickered back up to my face, searching for the truth in it. "Always? I find that hard to believe."

"Always." I drew her close and caught her mouth with mine, giving her a firm kiss. Her hands slid around my neck and her body pressed close, waking up parts of me that had been long neglected. I'd been celibate since Faya had left me eight years ago, but soon that would change. I couldn't deny I was looking forward to it, especially because it was Kira. She was the first woman I'd wanted after Faya broke my heart, and I wasn't going to let her go. Even if it meant sharing her with the other men. I'd find a way to accept it somehow...because I had to. Kira was my destiny, and that meant the other men were my destiny too.

And she was worth it.

6

KIRA

As we flew across the sky, I thought about what Slade had revealed this morning. I understood now why he had such a problem with the idea of sharing me with the other men. Not only had he grown up in the Earth Realm, but he'd been betrayed by the woman he'd loved. Faya had tried to cover up for her mistake by claiming she still loved Slade and wanted to be with both men, but if she'd known Slade for so many years then she must have known that would never work. Slade was the most loyal, dependable man I knew—and he expected the same from the ones he loved. When she'd cheated on him she'd broken his trust along with his heart, and there would be no return from that.

Our situation was completely different, and though he may understand that on an intellectual level, his heart was still wary. Underneath his tough exterior he worried he would be hurt again. I had to show him that would never happen with me. But even if I did somehow, could Slade ever really love someone again? Or had his past relationship with Faya robbed him of that forever?

We stopped for a quick lunch, where we ate most of our reserves of bread, cheese, dried fruit, and preserved meat. I sat apart from the men with Brin, who couldn't believe she'd slept through the entire bandit encounter and had me repeat the story for her three times, before asking a hundred questions about my past.

"They lived in the Air Realm back then," I said, before biting off a piece of beef jerky. "Cadock rescued me. That's how I met him."

"Rescued you from what?" she asked, as she brushed a bug off her trousers.

"I stopped in a small village looking for work. By then I'd been on the road for a year by myself and coin wasn't easy for me to come by. I didn't have a lot of useful skills, and I'd become pretty desperate for some food and shelter. Two men caught me and tried to kidnap me. I think they wanted to sell me." I shuddered at the memory. "Cadock killed the men and saved my life. His father's gang took me in and taught me much of what I know now. If it weren't for them, I'd probably be dead by now. Or worse."

"Lucky for us that he found you," Brin said. "But I'm surprised you left."

"It's hard to explain, but as I grew older I began to feel like my place was somewhere else. And though I cared about Cadock a lot, I knew it was time to move on." I shrugged. "Maybe the Gods were whispering in my ear that my destiny was with four other men."

Brin sighed. "I can't believe I slept through it all. I always miss the excitement."

I leaned back and gazed up at the cloudless blue sky. "Don't worry, I have a feeling there's a lot more ahead of us. Starting with this Resistance base."

"You think we'll find trouble there?"

"I hope not. I don't know much about them though, and Slade is worried."

"I know little about the Resistance beyond rumors and whispers. I can't imagine they'd be a problem though. After all, you want the same thing as them." She patted my hand. "You have nothing to worry about. And if it does turn out to be a trap, I've got your back."

"I hope you're right." I smiled at her. "I'm so grateful you came with us on this journey."

"I wouldn't miss it for anything. I only wish I could be of more help." She shrugged. "When surrounded by people who can use magic and turn into dragons, it's hard to be useful."

"You help me keep my sanity, give me a break from my overbearing men, and let me vent to you about whatever is bothering me. That's more important than anything else."

She let out a delightful little laugh. "Yes, that is what friends are for, and I can see how you might need an escape sometimes. Very well then, what's troubling you these days?"

I bit my lip, then made myself ask, "You've had multiple lovers at one time before, haven't you?"

"I have..." she said, her voice laced with interest.

"How do you make sure you're giving each one enough attention?"

"I had a very detailed calendar," she said with a wink. "But truly, it's all about balance and being in tune with their needs and feelings. I'm sure you'll figure it out in time."

I wasn't so sure about that. I glanced over at Slade, who was shaking his head at something Jasin was saying. "What do you do when one of them isn't happy with sharing you?"

A frown graced her red lips as she followed my gaze. "Sadly, I'm not sure there is anything to be done. It usually ends up with one of you ending the arrangement."

I sighed. "In our case that isn't an option."

"Then I suppose you both need to find a way to ensure you're all happy. Communication and honesty is the best bet. If you love each other, you'll make it work."

If only it were so easy. Slade said he cared about me, yes, but love was another thing entirely.

We rejoined the others and took off again on our dragon steeds, and soon the terrain became familiar. My excitement and anticipation grew with each farm and hill we went over, every one bringing us closer to Stoneham—and to Tash. Brin was a good friend, but I'd only recently met her and we came from completely opposite worlds. She'd grown up among the nobility and was practically a princess herself. Tash, on the other hand, had been like a sister to me for years. Her family had taken me in and given me a home and a job when I'd been desperate to settle down somewhere, and she'd mended my bruised soul with her kind smile and warm heart. She was the first person I'd told about being the Black Dragon, and I couldn't wait to catch up with her again soon. I wanted to know all about how she was doing after her father's death, and learn how the inn was faring now that she was running it.

As we approached Stoneham, I eagerly gazed across the forest where I used to hunt, until I saw something strange. Parts of the forest had turned black, the trees turned to cinder, the leaves now ash. It started with a few small patches, but then it spread as we grew closer to the village, until there was nothing left of the forest but death and decay.

My hands gripped Auric's scales harder and I yelled, "Hurry!"

Auric and Jasin pushed harder, their wings beating at the air, and the burnt remains of the forest gave way to a much worse scene. And no matter how fast we flew, it was already too late.

All that remained of Stoneham were ruins. Homes and

shops had become crumbled, blackened husks, and there was not a single living person in sight. The ground had split open right through the middle of the village, tearing apart the lives of everyone in it, and fire had finished them off.

Emotion choked my throat as Auric landed and I jumped off his back. The heady smell of lingering smoke clogged my nose as I ran down the road, but it didn't stop me from yelling out, "Tash? Launa? Anyone?"

Brin called out my name, but I ignored it. The others hung back as they took in the destruction, but I had to get closer to be sure it was real. I stumbled through the ruins in a daze, calling out for the people I once knew. Charred wood scattered the ground, which had turned thick and black, similar to the area around the Fire Temple's volcano where lava had once flowed. A few scattered bones poked through the black debris, but that was all I could find of the town's inhabitants.

A picture began to form in my mind of what had happened. Sark hadn't been the only Dragon who'd done this—this time he'd had help. The Jade Dragon had torn apart the very ground under the town, causing many of the buildings to collapse before Sark had set fire to them. Lava had risen up out of the deep trench and spread to envelop much of the town, and Sark had made sure anything it didn't touch was turned to cinders. There was nothing left.

Had anyone made it out alive? Or had Sark chased them down and roasted them one by one? Was that what those patches of fire were in the forest? My stomach churned at the thought, and I swallowed down bile as I continued forward.

At the edge of the village I found the rubble that had once been the inn—my home for the last few years. Some other buildings had partially survived, though they'd never be able to be salvaged, but not this one. It had been so thoroughly destroyed it was impossible to tell it had once been a two-story inn teeming with life. Now all that remained was a black crater in the earth.

I moved forward anyway, my heart unwilling to accept what my eyes clearly saw or the acrid scent in my nose. My boot struck something hard in the ash, and I glanced down at it. Something white stood out from the debris. A bone.

I bent down and touched the pale white surface, and revulsion instantly spread through me. I felt the lack of life within the bone keenly, and it made me want to yank my hand away. Death was the opposite of my spirit magic, and being so close to it tore at my soul. And worst of all, I could sense who this bone had once belonged to.

"Tash!" I cried out, my throat burning. I sank to my knees, instantly coating them in thick black soot, as tears streamed down my face. She couldn't be gone. None of this was real. It was a bad dream, a nightmare my mind had conjured up using memories of my parents' deaths, when Sark had burned our home alive with them trapped inside. Except every one of my senses told me this was real, from the air I choked on, to the ash on my skin, to the bitter taste in my mouth. The bone in front of me was undeniable proof. I just didn't want to believe it.

The people in Stoneham were innocent. Tash was the kindest girl I'd ever known. And now they were gone. Forever.

All because of me.

7

REVEN

I slid off of Jasin's scaled back while Kira dashed through the ruined town. Slade started after her, but I stopped him with an arm across his chest. "Give her a moment."

He scowled, but reluctantly nodded as Kira slipped away. I keenly remembered coming home to a scene like this, and the shock and horror that came with it. There was nothing we could do for her until she had a few minutes to process what she was seeing. She'd lived through this before too and she was strong. She simply needed time.

Jasin growled as he looked around. "How could they do this?"

"This is what they do," I said, willing my voice to be hard to keep it from wavering. "We've seen it before."

"Never on this scale," Auric said, turning to face me. "Doesn't it bother you?"

I crossed my arms and ignored his question. Of course it

bothered me, more than they knew, but I couldn't show that side to them. If I let one crack break through my cool exterior, I'd fall apart completely. The memories would come rushing back and they would wear me down until I was nothing but a husk, like those buildings in front of us. I wasn't going to let that happen, not when Kira might need me.

"These poor people," Brin said, clutching her hands to her chest. "They never stood a chance."

"Someone might have escaped," Slade said.

Jasin nodded, standing taller now that he'd found a purpose. "We should look for signs of survivors. Auric and I can scout the surrounding area from the sky, while the rest of you can search the town itself."

Fools. There were no survivors, that was obvious. They just needed something productive to focus on to make them feel less helpless at the sight of so much death and destruction. I knew what that was like, so I let them carry on without voicing what a waste of time it would be.

Auric and Jasin took off into the air while Brin and Slade carefully examined some of the rubble. Once they were gone I picked my way through the debris, following Kira's path to the end of the town. I spotted her kneeling in front of what was once the inn she'd worked at, and now was nothing more than ash and bone. I really should give her a few more minutes alone, but something tugged at me, urging me to join her. If anyone knew what she was going through, it was me.

Kira didn't stir when I approached, even when I rested a hand on her shoulder. She simply stared at the place that had once been her home, her arms hanging listless at her sides, her knees pressing into the blackened ground. Dirty tears stained her face, and I resisted the impulse to wipe them away.

"The others are searching for survivors," I said quietly.

She finally looked up at me with haunted eyes. "But not you."

"We both know the Dragons wouldn't leave anyone alive." Unlike the others, Kira and I had seen this before. We'd both lost our families to the Crimson Dragon's fire, and we knew how he worked. But her face crumpled in response to my words, and I wondered if she'd held onto some hope that her friend was still alive. I was a complete ass. "I'm sorry, Kira."

"This is my fault," she whispered. "This wasn't random. The people here weren't part of the Resistance. They're dead because of *me*."

"They're dead because the Dragons are cruel, heartless bastards who think nothing of destroying lives." Gods, how did I always end up as the one who comforted her? One of the other guys should be doing this. Even Slade would be better than me. I wracked my brain, trying to think of something I could say to make her feel better. "For all we know, the Dragons had problems with the town that had nothing to do with you."

She shook her head at my feeble attempt, and though we

didn't share a bond yet, the guilt and heartbreak were clear on her face. "I led them here by sending Tash that letter. The Dragons must have intercepted it and guessed we'd stop here while we traveled through the Earth Realm. They did this to leave us a message that this is the price of opposing the Dragons. They won't simply destroy us— they'll destroy everyone we love."

I couldn't deny what she was saying since it was probably the truth, but if I let her sink into this kind of grief she might never come out of it. She blamed herself for what the Dragons had done, and that guilt would crush her spirit and make her want to give up entirely. I knew that all too well from experience.

Kira was the next Black Dragon and we needed her to be strong. She had to keep fighting. She had to rise above this and move forward. We needed her—and so did the world.

"And how are you going to respond?" I asked, making my tone hard.

Her head snapped up. "What?"

I narrowed my eyes at her. "You're the next Black Dragon, aren't you? Are you going to sit back and do nothing? Are you going to let them do this again to another town? Another family? Maybe Auric's, or Slade's?"

"No!" she cried, her hands clenching into fists.

"Then what are you going to do about it?"

She rose to her feet and wiped away the last of her tears. Resolve straightened her shoulders and made her stand taller. Determination tilted her chin up, and anger made her eyes turn to deadly slits. I watched the transformation take hold of her, turning her from victim to avenger in the space of seconds.

When she spoke, her voice was like ice and I heard the steel behind it. "I'm going to stop them."

"Yes, you are." I didn't doubt it for a second.

She stared into the ruins of her village one last time, before turning to me with an unforgiving look that made me wonder if I'd pushed her too far. "And then I'll make them pay for what they've done."

8

KIRA

W e buried what bones we could find, until all of us were covered in soot and the day grew late. I decorated Tash's grave with a few flowers Brin brought me and then stood over it for a long time, silently saying my goodbyes while the biting wind tore tears from my eyes. My mates stood behind me, giving me space, until it was time for us to go.

As we left Stoneham, the only thing that held me together was the thought of vengeance and retribution. The Dragons had taken so much from me over the course of my life, but no longer. I'd been on the run for so long, hiding from my destiny, but now I was ready to fight back. I was going to destroy them—or die trying.

We left the ruins of Stoneham behind and found another spot in the forest for us to camp for the night. A few of the others visited a nearby town for supplies and warmer clothes, but I didn't join them. I wouldn't put any more innocent people at risk with my presence.

As we set up camp, the others kept trying to comfort me or ask how I was doing, but I told them to leave me alone. Nothing they said or did could make this any easier or bring Tash back. The only thing that would ease the unrelenting ache in my chest was the death of all five Dragons before they could hurt anyone else.

I ate something—I had no idea what—and then visited the nearby river to clean myself off, although my movements were routine and my mind was barely there. The anger faded and I went completely numb for a while, until I remembered Tash again. The grief became so strong it made me double over. She was *gone*. I would never again see her smile, or hear her laugh, or eat her food. We'd never get to catch up on the last few months we'd been apart. The Dragons had taken her from me, and she was never coming back.

I'd lost so many people in my life that it should have gotten easier to lose another, but it never did. I doubted it ever would. I let the pain wrap around me and turn back into anger, filling me with red hot clarity. I had no one left except the people with me now, but none of my mates' families were safe while the Dragons were alive. We had no choice but to stop them.

Jasin stepped between the trees as he approached the river. "Kira?"

"Not now," I said. "I'd like to be alone."

"Are you sure?" he asked, his voice even closer.

"Just leave me be!" The words came out in a rush, and I immediately regretted my harsh tone. Jasin was only trying to help, but I couldn't deal with him right now, or anyone else for that matter. A tangled mix of emotions threatened to choke me—overwhelming grief, fiery anger, and crushing guilt for being the cause of all of this mess—and I rushed to my tent to get away.

But when I slipped inside, I found someone else waiting for me. An elderly woman with white hair, wrinkled skin, and eyes like steel. Enva. The strange woman who'd appeared to me ever since my twentieth birthday, when all of this had started. She always offered a few hints and tidbits of information, then vanished and left me with more questions than I'd had before.

"What are you doing here?" I asked. To say I wasn't in the mood to entertain her cryptic advice tonight was an understatement.

"I sensed that you had questions."

I cast her a sharp glare. "I always have questions, but I've had a rough day. This isn't a good time."

She studied me as I sat across from her. "Yes, I know. I'm sorry about your friend and your village. Being a Dragon can be a great burden sometimes."

"How would you know?" I snarled.

She gave me a sad smile. "I was one too, once. Many years ago."

My annoyance at her presence instantly vanished. "You were?"

"I suppose it's time you learned the truth." She folded her wrinkled hands in her lap. "Kira, I'm your grandmother."

I gaped at her. "My grandmother."

"Yes. Nysa, the Black Dragon, is my daughter."

"You mean..." I swallowed, trying to wrap my head around her words. "So it's true. The Black Dragon really is my mother?"

"She is."

I stared at the old woman before me, looking at her in a new light. My *grandmother*. A sense of rightness settled in my chest, and I knew it was true. "And you were the Black Dragon before her?"

"I was, although I was known as the White Dragon."

I blinked. "I didn't know we could be anything else."

She pursed her lips. "Yes, well, there's a lot you don't know. Much of that is Nysa's fault. She had all of our family's history destroyed, along with all information about previous Dragons. It's a miracle she let people remember the Gods, but even she can't wipe all traces of them from the world."

I had so many questions I didn't know where to start. I wanted to know about her time as the White Dragon, and how it had led to Nysa becoming the Black Dragon and ruling for so long. But instead I found myself asking, "How are you here? Aren't you over a thousand years old at this point?"

"I would be. Assuming I was still alive." She waved away my questioning look. "I died a long time ago, but I'm trapped between life and death. My connection to the Spirit Goddess and my magic lets me watch over you and sometimes manifest for a brief period, although it takes a lot out of me so I can't stay for long."

"Why are you trapped?"

She pursed her lips before responding. "That is a longer tale, which needs to wait for another visit. The short version is that the way to the afterlife has been closed for the last thousand years. Everyone who dies is trapped—not only me."

"Everyone?" Horror crept over me as I imagined how many people that would be after all this time. And now Tash was one of them, along with everyone else I'd known in the village. "So those souls that can't find peace...is there any way to save them?"

"There is. You must defeat Nysa."

Easier said than done. I'd been determined to stop the Dragons earlier, but now my task seemed even more challenging. "Does she control the shades?"

"Yes, she does."

As I suspected. I dragged a hand through my hair. "What about the elementals?"

"No. The elementals hate both the Dragons and the shades."

Finally, a small bit of good news. I rubbed my eyes, suddenly exhausted. "How am I supposed to defeat her and the other Dragons? They're so much more powerful than we are."

"I've noticed." She snorted. "You need to train more. Now that you have two bonded mates, practice combining their elements."

"Combining...how?"

She rolled her eyes up at the roof of the tent like I was a complete fool. "Fire and earth together make lava. Water and air make fog. It's all fairly obvious."

I nodded slowly. "And fire and air make lightning."

"Exactly. Your mates will be able to combine their magic through their connection with you. Then you'll all be able to summon the joint elements."

That explained how the Dragons had summoned lightning during our fight at the Air Temple, and how Stoneham had been covered in lava. If we could figure out how to combine our magic in such a way we might have a chance. Or at least more of a chance than we had now.

"I wish I could tell you more, but the other side pulls at me already." She pressed a wrinkled hand to my cheek and stared into my eyes. "Stay strong, Kira. The journey is long and fraught with danger, but you're on the right path. Keep going and you'll find your way."

I pressed my hand against hers, wishing she didn't have to leave. It wasn't fair that as soon as I'd found another member of my family, I was losing her again. "I will...grandmother."

She faded away before my eyes, until it was like she had never been in the tent at all. I rubbed my weary face and thought on her words. I'd tried to deny that the Black Dragon was my mother, hoping it hadn't been true, even when my gut had told me it was. There was no denying it any longer, but that didn't mean I had to become her either. Enva, the White Dragon, had proved that. She had been helping me all this time, so she must disapprove of her daughter's actions and wanted Nysa stopped too. That couldn't be easy for her, but perhaps she'd grown tired of watching the world tumble into chaos and had to do something to help stop it. I'd have to ask her at her next visit, whenever that would be. I shuddered at the thought of her trapped between life and death, along with all those other people. Nysa must be the cause of it somehow, if stopping her would put an end to it.

At least now I had an idea of what to focus on: figuring out how to combine the elements.

9
AURIC

Kira's eyes burned with determination as she stood before us. "We need to make lightning."

It was the morning after we'd discovered Stoneham had been destroyed, and she'd told all of us about her visit from Enva while we'd had some bread and cheese. Then she'd insisted Jasin and I train with her immediately while the others prepared for us to depart. The tone in her voice had left no room for argument, and now she stood before us with her hands clenched in fists, her shoulders stiff, and a fierce slant to her lips.

All night long I'd tossed and turned, worrying about how she was doing and wishing I could comfort her, but she'd made it clear she wanted to be alone. Any time one of us tried to talk to her—and we'd all tried—she'd sent us away. Now I wondered if I should have tried more. I wasn't sure I liked this new, rage-filled Kira that had emerged after she'd spoken with Reven. Gods only knew what he'd said to her to make her turn her grief into fury. I'd never seen her like this before and wasn't sure what to make of it...or how to undo it.

Jasin arched an eyebrow at her. "And how are we supposed to do that?"

My brow furrowed. "Yes, you said we needed to combine the elements, but it doesn't seem like Enva gave us any actual information on how to do that."

Kira crossed her arms. "It must not be that hard to figure out. We'll just have to try."

I sighed and looked over at Jasin, who shrugged. We stood near the river we'd camped beside, away from the others and within reach of water in case things went wrong during training. I summoned a ball of swirling air in my palm, while Jasin did the same with fire. We moved closer and raised our hands to combine the two elements together —but all it did was snuff them both out.

"Well, that didn't work," Jasin said. "Now what?"

"Maybe I need to do it," Kira said. She summoned both elements in her hands and tried to force them together, with the same result. We'd been practicing with air in the few moments we could find since we'd left the temple, and she'd picked up the basics of controlling it quickly. I sensed she found it easier—or less intimidating—than fire. Of course, it would take a lot more training before she was a master. After all, I was still learning new things every day, including lightning it seemed.

"Gods!" Kira yelled, as the elements disappeared from

her hands. Her eyes filled with tears and she wiped them away with quick, angry strokes. She was trying to mask her grief by channeling it into fury and action, but it was still there under the surface. She would have to deal with it at some point, but not today I supposed.

"We'll get it eventually," I reassured her. "What else can we try?"

"I don't know." She turned away, her face twisted with frustration. I hated seeing her like this, but wasn't sure what to do.

"Remind us again what Enva told you," Jasin said, in a tone one usually reserved for trying to calm a wild animal. I could tell this was tearing him apart too.

Kira scowled. "She said you'll be able to combine your magic through your connection with me."

I nodded slowly as I considered her words. "Maybe she doesn't mean we should literally combine them, but somehow access the other's element through our bond."

"Is that possible?" Jasin asked.

I spread my hands. "Your guess is as good as mine."

"Can you feel each other through the bond like I feel the two of you?" Kira asked.

I shook my head. "Not that I've noticed, but my bond with you is still so new. I'm only beginning to feel your presence."

"It gets stronger when we're touching," Kira said. She reached for both our hands, linking the three of us together. From the corner of my eye I saw Slade, Reven, and Brin packing our things and giving us curious looks. They had to be worried about Kira too, but they knew better than to interrupt us during training.

My bond with Kira burst inside me at her touch, much stronger than it had ever been before. Waves of grief, anger, and guilt washed over me and it took me a moment to realize they were coming from her, along with a sense of desperation and determination, plus a dash of frustration and impatience. I sucked in a sharp breath as I sorted through her emotions and found my way back to my own self again.

"I think I can feel Auric through the bond," Jasin said. "But it's very faint."

When I glanced over, his eyes were closed. I copied him and searched through that tangled web that was my sense of Kira and there, in the distance, was a small flickering flame that felt like Jasin.

"I sense you too, but only barely," I said.

"Try to access each other's magic," Kira said.

I reached through the bond for Jasin's flame, but it was faint and elusive. I felt a slight tug inside me and wondered if it was him doing the same. We faced the river and in front of us the air shimmered with a slight buzzing sound, like a spark being struck. Kira's face tightened and her hand gripped mine harder, but then the sound vanished. We'd lost it.

Sweat beaded on Jasin's forehead. "Almost got it, but the bond is still too weak."

"Maybe it will get stronger with time," I said. "The Dragons have been bonded for hundreds of years, after all."

"We don't have time!" Kira said, obviously exasperated. She dropped our hands and pinched the bridge of her nose. I longed to pull her into my arms and tell her everything would be all right, but I knew she would only push me away right now.

"We'll keep trying until we get it," Jasin said.

Slade trudged through the brush toward us and called out, "We're ready to leave when you are."

Kira sighed. "I suppose we should get going if we're going to reach the Resistance by nightfall."

I rested a hand on her back. "It was only our first attempt. We'll get there eventually."

We began to follow Slade back to the camp, when a loud splash caught our attention. We froze and turned toward the river, my magic rising as I prepared to defend against a potential threat, and I felt Jasin do the same. Reven and Brin rushed to our sides, both holding their swords and ready for battle. Kira stood in front of us, facing the river like a warrior queen as she slowly drew her sword.

If the Dragons had found us, we weren't going down without a fight.

10

KIRA

The river was wide and flowing fast, and farther down it something large flailed about in the water as if drowning. I couldn't make out what it was—an animal or a big man perhaps—but it seemed to be fighting against a rock, or perhaps holding onto it. No, I realized as it drew closer, the thing splashing about *was* the rock.

"It's an elemental!" Auric said with a gasp.

Jasin immediately summoned fire into his palms. The only way to stop elementals was with magic—we'd learned that when a group of water ones had attacked our boat while we were at sea. But this elemental didn't appear to be attacking us—it seemed to be in trouble.

"It's small for a rock elemental," Slade said.

As its stony head burst above the water and tried to drag in a breath, I realized why it was so small. I dashed toward the river, leaving the others no choice but to follow. "It's a child!"

"What are you doing?" Jasin asked, as he trampled through the brush behind me.

"We have to save it!" I called over my shoulder. The small elemental was clearly drowning, it's body too heavy and dense for it to stay afloat. It must have fallen in the river, and there didn't seem to be any other elementals around to rescue it. If we didn't help, it would die.

We reached the edge of the river where the elemental struggled against the current. My mates spread out around me, still wary, while I tried to figure out a rescue plan.

"This isn't safe," Slade muttered.

Auric nodded. "If there's one elemental here, there must be others nearby."

"For all we know this is a trap," Reven said, crossing his arms.

"I don't care. We have to help it." I knew I was taking a big risk, but I wasn't letting a child die on my watch, whether it was human, animal, or elemental. "Reven, use your magic to rescue it."

He scowled, but made a lazy gesture toward the river. The water changed from rushing past us to slowly creeping forward. While the current brought the elemental closer to us, Jasin and Auric watched the trees for an attack. I waded out into the river and tried to grab hold of the elemental's rocky body, but it let out a terrible sound, like steel scraping against stone.

"It's okay, we're trying to help," I told it. I had no idea if it could understand me, but hopefully the sound of my voice would show I wasn't a threat. The elemental's glowing eyes widened, but when I reached for it again it didn't fight back. But I couldn't move it on my own—the elemental was nearly as big as I was and a lot heavier than I expected, even though it was small for its kind. Slade jumped into the water next to me and grabbed the other side of the elemental, and together we heaved it out of the river and onto the grassy banks.

The elemental coughed and water ran out of its mouth, its eyes still huge and glowing bright gold. I tried to pat it on its back, but wasn't sure if it had lungs or not—it seemed to be made entirely of thick, gray stone. Now that it was out of the water I could see it had a large, rounded chest that made up most of its bulk, along with two thick arms and short, stumpy legs.

"You're all right now," I said to it, as I kept patting its hard back. The elemental was shaking, but it didn't try to escape, so it must have sensed we weren't going to harm it. The others kept their hands near their weapons, but they wouldn't attack unless they thought I was in danger.

Movement caught our attention, and four much larger rock elementals emerged from the trees down the river. They moved surprisingly fast considering their squat legs, and their glowing eyes fixed on us with obvious malice. Brin and my mates tensed beside me, sensing a looming fight, but Enva's words last night gave me the idea to approach this differently. If the elementals weren't working for the Black

Dragon, that meant they didn't need to be our enemies... assuming I could reach them somehow.

"Don't attack," I said to my mates quietly. "I want to talk to them."

"Talk?" Jasin snorted. "Elementals don't talk. They attack."

"I want to try."

I helped the elemental child to its feet, making sure it could stand on its own. It suddenly spotted the other elementals and let out that strange sound again, then rushed toward them. The larger elementals quickly surrounded it, as if making sure it was all right. I walked toward them slowly, waving for my mates to stay back. This would have to be handled carefully, or it would all go wrong...and we would likely only have one chance.

One of the elementals broke apart and faced me. Its face was stony and incomprehensible, with a gaping mouth full of jagged rock and those eerie glowing eyes. We stared at each other without moving, and then it asked, "Why did you help him, Spirit Dragon?"

The voice that came from the elemental was like the deep rumble of an earthquake, and the words were spoken slowly, as if it wasn't used to our language—but it was speaking. My heart leaped at the knowledge we could communicate with them.

"I didn't want him to drown," I said. "We mean your kind no harm. We only want to talk."

"We are no friend to the Dragons," he grumbled.

"We're not like the other Dragons. We want to stop them and restore balance to the world. A world where both humans and elementals can live in peace together."

"Perhaps," the elemental said, obviously unconvinced.

The other elementals were now watching us, and the small one made a sound I didn't understand. One of the others replied, and they carried on for a few seconds in their gravelly language while I looked on. The leader rumbled something back at them, before turning to me again.

"We are in your debt, Spirit Dragon." The elemental did not sound pleased about that, but it was hard to tell with its strange voice. I was too surprised to respond immediately, and then it was too late, as they all stomped back into the forest.

"That was incredible," Auric said, moving to my side. "I had no idea the elementals could speak our language. I need to record this immediately."

Jasin put out the fire in his hands. "It was still risky helping them. They nearly attacked us even after we saved that little one."

"Yes, but it was worth it," I replied. "Now we know they can communicate with us, and if they hate the other Dragons as much as Enva said, we might be able to convince them to become our allies."

"That seems unlikely," Reven said.

Slade rubbed his beard. "It's worth trying."

"Kira will make it happen," Brin said. "Especially now that they owe her."

I stared after the elementals for another moment, then turned toward my team. "We'll worry about that another day. Right now we need to find the Resistance."

11

JASIN

Auric pointed one of his talons at a mountain in the distance and I nodded. We both tilted our wings slightly to adjust our course, and exhilaration took hold as the brisk wind rushed over my scales.

Being a dragon was incredible. I could fly for hours without growing tired, cross great distances faster than any horse, and was stronger than ever before. Even with Slade and Brin on my back, along with half of our supplies and equipment, I barely noticed the weight. And with fire burning in my lungs, along with my sharp talons and fangs, I could defend Kira better than I could before.

Auric and I flew closer to the snow-capped mountains, and the air around us grew colder. We knew from Cadock's mark on the map that the Resistance base was somewhere on the edge of these mountains in a cave, and he'd instructed us to look for a rock in the shape of two breasts, but so far we hadn't spotted them.

"There," Brin said, from my back. Her arm stretched over my right wing and I followed it's direction to the base of a mountain where two large, rounded boulders pointed at the sky. I didn't see an entrance, but assumed it would become more obvious once we got closer.

Auric and I swooped down into a nearby forest and found a good spot to land, since showing up as dragons probably wouldn't elicit a good reaction. Once on the ground, we hid anything we couldn't carry and then began the trek to the mountain. None of us felt like talking much with the memory of Kira's village still fresh in our minds, along with that dangerous encounter with the elementals. Kira thought she might be able to convince them to help us, but I wasn't sure even she could reverse hundreds of years of conflict and turn it into an alliance.

When we reached the mountain range and stood beside the twin rocks, the way inside was no more clear. It wouldn't be a very good secret base if the entrance was obvious, but I'd hoped for something more than this. If that bandit had betrayed us or led us astray, I was going to track him down and make him pay.

"I didn't see an entrance while flying overhead," Auric said.

I glared up at the mountain. "Cadock probably lied to us. I bet he has no idea where the Resistance base is."

"He wouldn't do that," Kira said, as she pulled her cloak

around her to fight off the chill. "It's here. We just need to look for it."

"I can find it." Slade took a few steps forward and pressed his palm against the slope of the mountain. He closed his eyes and his face became calm, while we stood back and waited. He'd done this before and he'd always been able to find a cave, a lake, or whatever we were looking for with his magic. A useful trick indeed.

When he opened his eyes, he removed his hand and turned to us. "Follow me."

We began to climb the steep side of the mountain, and I longed to have my wings so I could simply fly up it. It didn't help that my steps were dragging and hesitant either. I wasn't exactly thrilled to be going into the Resistance base, and had no desire to get there any faster, even if it was what Kira wanted.

When I'd been part of the Onyx Army I'd committed horrible acts against the Resistance in the name of duty. I'd helped slaughter entire villages thought to be harboring their members even though it had made me sick. Disobeying my orders had never been an option, no matter how much I'd secretly questioned my superiors. At the time, I'd tried to justify my actions because my brother had been killed by the Resistance, or by telling myself that the Dragons knew what had to be done to keep the world safe. Now I knew better. The guilt and regret tore at me with every step, and I'd do anything to go back and reverse the damage I'd caused and bring back the lives I'd cut short.

When we'd visited the Fire Realm we'd rescued a few prisoners from execution and escorted them to safety, but one of them had recognized me from my past crimes. She'd been terrified of me, and I couldn't blame her for her reaction, even if it had made me feel like the worst human being in all the four Realms.

Now I was about to face those people again, and would be forced to look into their eyes knowing I'd once been their enemy and their executioner. I liked to think that I'd changed and that I could atone for my sins by stopping the other Dragons, but I wasn't sure I could ever make up for my mistakes. All I could do was stand by Kira's side and try to be a better man in the future.

Slade stopped about halfway up the mountainside and found a small crevice that was nearly impossible to see due to the shape of the rocks around it. "I think this is it."

He slipped through the crack, and the rest of us had to follow one by one. A very defensible entrance since you could easily pick off people as they entered. I rested my hand on my sword in case there was trouble.

Through the crevice, the stone opened up to a wider cave and we spread out inside it. A large metal door stood in front of us and Kira approached it, paused for a moment, and then banged on it sharply three times.

After a brief wait, two heavily armed guards stepped out of the door, before it slammed shut behind them again. They pointed swords at us as one said, "State your business here."

We all glanced at Kira, who stood at the front of our

group. "We're here to speak with the leader of the Resistance," she said. "Parin."

"There's no Resistance here," the female guard said. "You should turn around and head back wherever you came from."

Kira stood tall and met the woman's gaze, her voice stern. "We know that isn't true, and we have information your people would definitely like to know about. We're here to help you fight the Dragons."

"And why should we believe you?" the male guard asked.

Kira's jaw clenched and she raised her hands, likely about to use her magic to prove who she was. But then the door opened behind the guards and a dark-skinned woman with hair cropped close to her head stepped out. She was lithe and beautiful, with a fierce intensity in her eyes that made me think she was not to be underestimated. A large sword hung from her hip, along with a dagger on the other.

"Slade?" she asked, her voice almost breathless as she stared at him. "Is that really you?"

Slade's jaw clenched and his brow furrowed. It was the most emotion I'd seen on his stony face in days. Maybe weeks. Whoever this woman was, he was not pleased to see her. "Hello, Faya."

"Gods, it is you." She pressed a hand to her chest, her brown eyes wide. "What are you doing here?"

"We need to speak with Parin," Kira said, her voice hard. She wasn't happy to see this woman either. Was this the girl Slade had loved and lost many years ago? That would explain a lot.

Faya blinked, and finally saw the rest of us standing there. "Of course. Come inside. I'll take you to Parin." She flashed Slade another questioning look. "And then we can catch up."

The guards lowered their weapons and allowed us to pass. Faya led us through the metal door and we stepped into a massive, domed space that took my breath away. The cave stretched for such a great distance that I couldn't see the end of it, while the dark gray stone slanted into a perfectly smooth ceiling high above us. Wooden and stone buildings filled the giant cave, laid out in a way so there were small roads running between them. More armed guards awaited us inside, while people walked about and gave us curious looks before continuing on to their destinations. Many of them were armed, but some looked like civilians. I even saw a small child running after a woman. This wasn't just a base, this was an entire village. And none of them screamed or cried out at the sight of me—maybe my past would truly stay behind me this time.

"Welcome to Slateden," Faya said. "Home of the Resistance."

"Impressive," I said. There was no hint from outside that any of this existed, but there must be hundreds of people living here.

"When did you do all this?" Slade asked.

"About five years ago. We realized we needed a more permanent base of operations, and one that was completely hidden from the world." She gave us all a sharp look. "It's a secret any one of us would die to protect."

I met her eyes with a hard look of my own. This was Slade's former fiancé, who had betrayed him with another man and abandoned him to join the Resistance. She'd hurt one of the men I cared about more than anything in the world, and even if we became allies I would never forgive her for that. And now she had the nerve to think we'd expose this place?

"We're honored to be welcomed inside," Auric said diplomatically.

"Your secret is safe with us," Jasin added.

Faya nodded and continued walking into the village, past small houses and shops. I fell into step behind her and sneaked a glance at Slade, whose face remained hard. It had to be uncomfortable for him to see Faya again, but he'd done a fine job of hiding it so far.

She led us to a wide, wooden building with a slanted roof and double doors. Guards were stationed outside of it, and they nodded at her as we stepped inside. The interior was sparse, as was the rest of Slateden from what I'd seen, favoring function over form. We walked up a narrow staircase, and then she knocked on a plain door.

"Come in," a voice called out from inside.

"Give me a moment," Faya told us, before slipping into the room and closing the door behind her. I exchanged awkward, anxious looks with my mates and Brin while we waited outside, but Faya emerged only a minute or two later and opened the door wide. "He'll see you now."

"I'll wait out here," Brin said, stepping back. It was part of our plan—she'd try to explore the base and learn what she could while the rest of us spoke with Parin.

We left her behind and stepped into the room, where a man sat behind a plain wooden desk with his hands folded upon it. His skin was dark like Slade's and Faya's, as was common in the Earth Realm, but his head was smooth and hairless, while his deep brown eyes took us in with a discerning look. He was probably in his mid-to-late thirties and attractive in a way that was both commanding and approachable. There was no doubt in my mind this was Parin, the Resistance leader.

"Slade, it's good to see you again," Parin said, although there was an edge to his voice that made me doubt his sincerity. Faya had moved to stand just behind his shoulder, and watched the exchange with interest.

"Parin," Slade replied, crossing his arms and setting his jaw.

"Who are your companions? I'm told they wish to speak with me?"

I stepped forward and introduced myself and the others before adding, "We've come to ask for your help."

Parin leaned back in his chair and his eyes took me in with curiosity. "And why should we help you?"

"We share a common goal—to overthrow the Dragons and free the people of their rule. We'd like to form an alliance with you."

He arched an eyebrow. "The five of you, and who else? Do you have an army? A spy network? What exactly can you offer?"

Anger threatened to rise up inside me, anger that had been all too close to the surface ever since I'd discovered Stoneham, but I clenched my fists and reminded myself that I had to be diplomatic if I wanted to win this man over. "No, we don't have any of those things. But we have something more powerful—the Gods' favor."

"The Gods?" Parin laughed. "The Gods sleep while the rest of the world spins into chaos."

"They sleep no longer," Slade said.

"How do you know that?" Faya asked.

"Because we've met them," Auric replied.

Both Faya and Parin appeared doubtful, and it was clear that words alone wouldn't convince them. "The Gods have chosen us as their new Dragons," I said, as I summoned balls of swirling fire and air into my palms. "I'm going to be the next Black Dragon, and these are my mates. We're planning to defeat the current Dragons and bring balance to the world—but we could use your help."

I expected shock or disbelief, since those were the normal reactions when I told people who we were or showed them my magic, but Parin's expression didn't change. Faya didn't react either, for that matter. I let the magic in my palms sputter and die out.

"Yes, we've heard about you," Parin said.

"You knew about us already?" Reven asked.

Parin nodded. "I've heard reports of the Dragons searching for five people matching your description, along with rumors of people who rescued Resistance members using the elements and strange Dragons flying the skies. I had a feeling you'd come see me at some point."

"Then you'll help us?" I asked.

"That I haven't decided." He drummed his fingers on

the table as he scrutinized us. "Yes, we both share a common goal—for now. But what happens if you do overthrow the Dragons and take their place? How do we know we aren't trading one dictatorship for another?"

"We have no interest in ruling," I said. "The Gods told us that the Dragons originally had another role—to keep the world in balance and to protect both humans and elementals. The individual Realms ruled themselves, and the Dragons traveled the world to assist where they could. Nysa and her Dragons took their role too far and somehow found a way to defy the Gods, attain immortality, and become rulers of this land. We plan to return the power to the leaders of the Realms and to the people, while we'll act only as peacekeepers and guardians. And when the time comes, we'll step down so other Dragons can take our place."

"A lofty plan, but forgive me if I find it hard to believe people could throw away all that power and control so easily. Especially the likes of you." His eyes swept over us, becoming hard. "Slade, who turned his back on the Resistance long ago. Jasin, a member of the Onyx Army who used to hunt down my own people. Auric, a prince whose father serves the Dragons. Reven, who was once the infamous assassin known as the Black Hood, if I'm not mistaken. And you, Kira. Once a bandit, and still little more than a child. And you truly think you can save us all?"

My back stiffened. Everything he'd said was true, and he'd mentioned things even I hadn't known, like Reven's assassin name...but he was wrong about us. "That's not who we are anymore. Where we began does not define what we will become. What matters now are the actions we take in the future."

"I've done terrible things in the past, as have many of us here," Jasin said, all the cockiness gone from his voice for once. "I can tell you that I've changed and that I wish to make things right now, but I understand if you don't believe me. I'm willing to take whatever justice you demand for my crimes, but please don't let my actions color your opinion of Kira, or stop you from helping her. My crimes are my own, as should be my punishment."

"None of us asked for this," Slade said, stepping forward until he stood at my side. "We all had lives we were forced to leave when the Gods chose us." He glanced at Faya. "But you know me. I wanted to spend the rest of my days as a simple blacksmith and had no plans to leave my village. But the Earth God sent me to find Kira, and we all became committed to her cause. None of us is doing this for the power or the glory."

"I believe you, Slade," Faya said, before turning to Parin. "And if Slade trusts these people, perhaps we should trust them as well."

"Perhaps." Parin studied me closer. "What exactly do you need help with?"

"We need to reach the Earth Temple and the Water Temple, but the Dragons know we'll be going to both," I said. "We assume they'll be waiting for us at each one, and we're not yet strong enough to defeat them. Any information or help you could provide would be greatly appreciated."

Parin and Faya exchanged a look that spoke volumes, though I wasn't sure what exactly passed between them. Eventually Parin stood and moved to the back wall, where he picked up a small green statue in the shape of a dragon. Made from jade, I assumed.

"My mother made this for me," Parin said, as he turned and offered it to me.

I took the tiny statue carefully and studied it. The craftsmanship was exquisite, from the talons and the fangs to the delicate scales. "She carved it?"

He smiled as I handed it back to him. "In a sense. She was the High Priestess of the Earth God."

"Did she make this cave too?" Auric asked.

"She did." He set the tiny dragon back down and faced us again. "Many years ago, when I was a young man of seventeen years, she met with the Fire God's High Priestess and was told that new Dragons would arise to defeat the current ones. My mother was skeptical, but she tasked me and my sister with the duty of preparing for an upcoming battle anyway. My sister trained to become the next High Priestess, while I joined the Resistance. Back then it was small and lacked firm leadership. I rose through the ranks and eventually was voted in as leader." He spread his hands. "And now here we are, at the moment I've spent my life preparing for, and I only wish my mother could have lived to see this moment herself."

"I'm sorry," I said, my stomach sinking. "Can I ask what happened to her?"

His hands slowly formed into fists. "The Dragons recently paid a visit to the Earth Temple and left no one alive."

I bowed my head and swallowed back my fury. "They did the same thing at the Air Temple. I'm so sorry. Is your sister...?"

He shook his head. "Thankfully my mother had already sent her away. She's in hiding now, but she's ready to take on the role of High Priestess when it's safe again."

"It won't be safe until the Dragons are gone," Jasin said. "They've become the enemies of the Gods and those who serve them."

"So it seems." Parin paused and then offered me his hand. "Yes, Kira, we will help you."

I clasped his hand briefly as relief flowed through me, taking away some of the tension in my limbs. "Thank you."

He gave a sharp nod. "I can get you inside the Temple without a problem—there are many secret tunnels, thanks to my mother, and even though it's been destroyed we should be able to gain access. But you're right that there are Dragons waiting for you. I received a report this morning that the Jade Dragon and the Crimson Dragon were both there and seemed to have no plans to leave. Even if we do get you inside, they'll never let you complete the bonding."

"We need a distraction," Reven said. "Can your people provide that?"

"They can, though it'll be dangerous. I hesitate to send my people into battle against an opponent they can't possibly win against."

"All we need is some time," I said. "And we can help. We have two Dragons of our own."

He nodded. "That does make the odds better. But we can discuss strategy in greater detail tomorrow. For now, you must be exhausted from your travels. My wife will show you to rooms where you can rest for the night, and I'll have some food sent up too."

"Thank you," I said, although I didn't miss the way he'd addressed Faya. Slade hadn't either, from the way his shoulders stiffened. This alliance could prove to be difficult for both of us, but it would be worth it if it meant defeating the Dragons. With the Resistance by our side, we might actually have a chance.

13

SLADE

An hour after we'd retreated to our guest rooms, a knock sounded on my door. I'd been preparing for bed and wore only my trousers, but I assumed it was Kira knocking and went to let her in. Instead I found Faya at my door.

She wore a thin gray dress that hugged her curves, her sword was gone, and her face was as lovely as I remembered, though her thick hair had been cut short and she looked like a mature woman now, instead of the fresh-faced girl I'd known. We'd both gained several years since we'd last seen each other.

My jaw clenched and I checked the hallway behind her to make sure we were alone. "You have some nerve coming here at this hour. And alone, too."

"I simply came to talk, nothing more," Faya said.

"We have nothing to talk about."

"Maybe you don't, but I do." She stepped forward, her voice low but genuine. "Slade, I'm sorry for what I did all those years ago. I know I hurt you terribly, and that was never my intention. I made so many mistakes back then."

I'd waited years to hear this apology, but now it was a little too late. I crossed my arms and leaned against the doorway. "Yes, you did."

"I understand if you can never forgive me, but I wanted to apologize anyway since we'll be working together. Parin said it was foolish, but I had to try to make this situation less awkward. There are bigger things at stake here than our feelings."

"That's the only reason I'm here," I said, my voice gruff. Everything about this encounter made me uncomfortable, but for Kira's sake I should try to get along with Faya and Parin. I forced myself to uncross my arms and loosen my shoulders. "When did you and Parin wed?"

"Six years ago."

"Are you happy?"

"I am. This is my place—at Parin's side." She gave me a slight smile. "And you? I can't imagine you were pleased about being chosen as one of Kira's mates."

"I wasn't at first, but I've come to accept my destiny."

Her smile widened as amusement danced in her eyes. "I always knew you were destined for greatness."

I snorted. "I never wanted greatness. I wanted a home, a family, and a warm meal on the table. Nothing more."

"So you say, but it was obvious to me that neither of us

was meant for a quiet life in Clayridge. We weren't meant for each other either." She paused as she studied my face. "Are you fond of her, at least?

"I am."

"Good. I hope one day you get your home and family with her, even if you'll never have a simple life." She reached up and touched my cheek, her fingers soft. "I want you to be happy too, Slade. Even if it's not with me."

A sense of peace settled over me. I touched her hand gently as it pressed against my cheek. "Thank you. And I'm sorry for everything I did too. I wasn't the perfect fiancé either."

A soft noise in the hallway caught my attention. I pulled away from Faya and peered around her to see if someone was there, but didn't spot anyone lurking about. I shook my head and stepped back, meeting Faya's eyes. "I appreciate your apology. Working together won't be a problem."

She inclined her head. "I'm glad to hear it. Have a good night, Slade."

"And you, Faya."

I shut the door and retreated back inside my room. It was small, little more than a bed with a table beside it, and the walls were rough, unfinished wood. The entire building housed traveling Resistance members when they stopped into Slateden, so it made sense there was nothing fancy about it, although the state of the wood did irritate me. Based on the construction of the building and most of the rest of the town, I guessed it had all been erected quickly and with the least amount of work or supplies.

Back when I'd helped the Resistance they'd had small camps that moved constantly to avoid detection, with other members hiding in different towns. I'd housed a few of them myself many times due to Faya's involvement with them.

Looking back, I should have seen that Faya would leave me for this life, and knew I should have cut her loose long ago. She'd never wanted to stay in Clayridge and be the wife of a blacksmith—she'd always had a need to fight. She'd broken my heart, betrayed my trust, and made me question whether I could love again—but seeing her today only made me realize it had all been for the best. She'd been my first love and an important part of my past, but she wasn't my future. Kira was—and I knew what I felt for her surpassed anything I'd once felt for Faya.

14

KIRA

S *he's touching his face.*

Pain lanced through me at the sight, especially when he didn't pull away. They spoke in low voices in his doorway and then he laid his hand over hers on his cheek. He wore no shirt, she wore a dress that left little to the imagination, and it was far too late for a social call. He should have sent her away, but instead he looked at her tenderly— and my heart broke.

I quickly rushed away, unable to stand the sight of them together for another second. Faya must have gone to Slade's room to rekindle their old romance and he hadn't sent her away. If I stayed longer would I watch him invite her inside? I couldn't bear the thought.

I'd visited the washroom and had decided to check on Slade to see how he was doing after seeing Faya again, but then I'd caught the two of them together. The anguish was so strong it was hard to see straight, and I reached for anger to steady me, like I'd done after Tash's death. How could Slade do this to me? Did he feel nothing for me at all? I was his mate. He was mine. *Mine.*

I found myself stumbling through the hallway away from the scene, but I didn't stop at my room. Instead I sharply banged on the one next to it.

Jasin opened the door with a grin. Like Slade, he wore only his trousers, and the sight of his naked chest ignited a fire inside me. His grin faded when he saw my face. "Kira, are you all right?"

"I want...I need..." I shook my head, unable to find the words to describe the turmoil inside me. I wanted to tear something apart with my bare hands. I wanted to lose myself for the rest of the night. I wanted someone to desire me as much as I desired them.

Somehow Jasin knew exactly what I needed, because he dragged me against him and slanted his mouth across mine. He kicked the door shut and I heard it bang behind us as I met his kiss with equal force, sliding my tongue against his. His hands were rough and demanding as they moved down my body, following my curves. I clutched his bare shoulders and pressed against him, craving his passion, his strength, his fire.

Warmth poured through me at his touch and I forgot everything but the heat of his lips and the feel of him against me. I ran my hands down his sculpted chest as my entire body sang with need for him. Through our bond I felt his lust rising too, along with his desire to claim me, please me, love me.

He pushed me back against the hard wall and his dark eyes met mine. I stared back at him, licking my lips, and he let out a low groan before taking my mouth again in a searing kiss. His hands moved down to yank my dress up to my thighs, baring me to him. I reached for the fall of his trousers at the same time and yanked them open. I was desperate to feel every hard inch of him inside me. There was no holding back, not tonight.

His fingers slipped between my legs, where he found my pulsing hot core already wet for him. My nipples tightened as he dipped between my folds, and I took hold of his cock in response. It strained toward me, hard, hot, and throbbing. His fingers plunged deep inside me, but I needed more. I needed all of him.

"Jasin," I gasped, as I lifted a leg to wrap around his hips, trying to bring him closer.

In response, he lifted me up and pinned me against the wall, aligning our bodies together. My back arched as he filled me completely, all the way to the hilt. We both groaned and clung to one another as we were joined, and I realized it was just the two of us for the first time since the Fire Temple. No Auric tonight, just me and my Crimson Dragon becoming one.

He planted a hand on the wall by my head while the other curved around my bottom, holding me in place as he began to thrust into me. My legs tightened around him and I moaned as his mouth moved to my neck. He took me with pure, unleashed need, and I couldn't get enough.

"Mine," I whispered, as I dug my nails into his behind, pulling him deeper into me. Jasin had been my first mate and he'd never wavered in his devotion to me. He'd loved me from the beginning...and he knew exactly how to drive me wild.

"Always." He slammed into me, claiming me as his mate too.

We fell into a passionate rhythm of push and pull, give and take, in and out. Soon there was no more talking, only heavy breathing as the friction between us built. My body seemed to wind tighter and tighter with each slide of his cock, and when he lifted me up higher to get a deeper angle, I fell apart. I clenched around him as pleasure pulsed through me, and I felt his own release only moments later, not just in my body but through our bond. He called out my name and buried himself in me one last time as his hot seed filled me.

Jasin brought his lips to mine again for a slow, loving kiss while we clung to each other and the last flames of passion faded. My heart pounded and I couldn't quite catch my breath, but the earlier tension was gone thanks to Jasin. He carried me to his bed and set me down in it, then wrapped his body around mine. He was so warm it was almost too much, but I couldn't bear the thought of moving away.

"I love you," he said, brushing his lips against my shoulder.

I relaxed against him even more. "I love you too."

"When you arrived you seemed upset. Do you want to talk?"

"No." I'd have to deal with Slade eventually, but not tonight. All I wanted now was to sleep next to my mate.

Jasin nodded and let it go, and that was why I'd come to him and no other. I'd wanted his fiery passion and the release he could bring, not Auric with his probing questions and kind eyes, or Reven with his cold voice and icy distance. Jasin had given me exactly what I'd needed, and now his love wrapped around me like a comforting blanket. The bond between us flared brighter than ever before, causing my emotions and his to become one big jumble of satisfaction and love.

It gave me an idea.

I turned in his arms to face him. "I think I know how to increase the bond between you and Auric. We need to invite him to bed again."

Jasin flashed a naughty grin as he brushed a piece of hair off my cheek. "Whatever my lady desires."

15

KIRA

Over the next day, my mates and I met with Parin, Faya, and other members of the Resistance to discuss strategy and make plans. Though I was ostensibly in charge among our group of Dragons, I felt comfortable leaving most of the decisions in this matter to my mates. Jasin had served in the Onyx Army for many years, Reven was an expert at stealth and infiltration, Auric was a fountain of knowledge, and Slade knew both the layout of the Earth Realm and the Resistance's inner workings. It'd be stupid now to ignore their expertise, and I was quite content to sit back and let them work, although I chimed in whenever I had an idea.

By the end of the day, we'd worked out a plan. In a week's time many members of the Resistance, along with Jasin and Auric, would ambush a large Onyx Army fort known as Salt Creek Tower. We believed a direct attack against such an important location would force any Dragons at the Earth Temple to come out to defend it, especially once they realized two of my mates were there too. The fort was close enough to the Earth Temple that the Dragons could fly there quickly, but not too close that it would be an obvious distraction. Once they were gone, Slade, Reven, and I would sneak through a back tunnel into the Earth Temple so we could complete the bonding. If Slade still wanted that.

I'd avoided him all day, and every time Faya spoke my stomach clenched tight. My mind kept drifting back to that image of the two of them standing together, before wondering what had occurred afterward. I tortured myself with thoughts of the two of them in bed together, and they only made my anger and misery grow.

But I couldn't avoid Slade forever.

It was late by the time we went back to our rooms, but I never made it to mine. Slade stopped me with a large hand on my shoulder. He turned me back to face him and my chest hardened.

"Is something wrong?" he asked. "You've been unable to meet my eyes all day."

My fists clenched at my side. "I saw you last night...with her."

Understanding dawned across his face. "She came to apologize. Nothing more."

"It looked like a lot more than that," I said, remembering the way he'd covered her hand with his own.

He shook his head. "We talked, that was all. We both

needed some closure so we could work together without any problems. But I swear, nothing happened."

My jaw clenched and I looked away. "How am I supposed to believe you?"

He took my chin and dragged my eyes back to his. Sometimes I forgot how unusually green they were, as if he'd been chosen by the Earth God from the moment he'd been conceived. "I haven't kissed a woman other than you in eight years. And that's the way I plan to keep it."

His lush mouth found mine and he gave me a kiss that left me with few doubts of his sincerity. Even when we'd first met I'd found myself staring at his full lips and wondered what it'd feel like with them against my own, and the reality was even better than I could have imagined. He coaxed my mouth open and worked magic with every stroke of his tongue, making me melt against him.

"I don't want Faya," he said against my lips. "Only you."

"Slade..." I pressed my forehead against his. I'd waited so long to hear those words from him and I wasn't prepared for the rush of emotions that swept through me when it finally happened.

He took my arm in his and moved us into my guest room, then softly shut the door. Once we were alone, he lovingly caressed my cheek as he gazed into my eyes. "Speaking with Faya only made me realize the depth of my feelings for you. I tried to deny them for so long, but I won't do it any longer. I can't."

"Finally," I said, as I pressed another kiss to his lips.

"Yes. I'm sorry it took me so long." He drew me into his arms and against his broad, muscular chest. I let my arms slide around his neck, clinging to him as the sensual kiss swept us both away. His long, hard length pressed against my stomach, and I groaned when I realized his desire mirrored my own.

His kisses made my knees weak, and I pulled us both down to sit on the bed. I needed to touch him, to taste him, to confirm he was mine. I gripped his shirt and dragged it up his chest, and our lips broke apart for only a few seconds as he helped me lift it off him. My hands splayed across his hard stomach, feeling the smooth ridges of his muscles and all the coiled power underneath. His skin was so dark against mine, and I loved the contrast between us. Hard and soft, dark and light, male and female—a perfect balance for each other.

He left a slow, delicious trail of kisses down my neck that had me aching for more. And when he pushed my dress off one shoulder and pressed his lips to my uncovered skin, I couldn't help but moan.

"I want you," I said, sliding my hands down to the hard bulge I'd felt earlier.

He caught my hand in his much larger one, stopping me from opening his trousers. "Not yet. Not until the Earth Temple."

An overwhelming need to be joined with Slade made it hard for me to think, to breathe, to live. "Please, I can't wait. Let me touch you at least."

He dragged my dress lower, until it freed one of my pale breasts. "When I finally take you, I want it to be in the Earth Temple before the Gods. I want everyone to know that I'm your mate for all eternity." His mouth continued lower, along the curve of my bosom. "But somehow I can't seem to stop myself."

"There are other things we can do," I said, as my hand moved to the back of his head, holding him against my chest.

He let out a low chuckle that vibrated against my skin. "Yes, there are."

He took the hard bud of my nipple between his lips then, making me gasp. His tongue slid along my sensitive skin, awakening every nerve in my body and sending a rush of heat between my thighs.

Just when it became almost too much, he tugged the other side of my dress down and began to lavish attention on that breast too. I threw my head back and succumbed to the pleasure of his mouth all over me, and the relief that came with knowing he wanted me as much as I wanted him. For so long I'd thought he wasn't interested in me romantically or sexually, that he was only with me out of duty and loyalty, but with every stroke of his tongue and sensual touch of his hands he showed me how wrong I'd been.

I dragged him back up to my lips, needing to kiss him again, and we fell back into the bed together. While our mouths collided, our hands slowly explored each other's bodies over our clothes. We touched each other like we had all the time in the world, so different from my encounter with Jasin last night, but just as satisfying.

While we kissed, my legs tangled with Slade's and my skirts inched their way up around my thighs. I felt one of his large hands settle on my bare skin just above my knees almost possessively, and I held my breath as he began to inch his way upward.

When his fingers drew close to my core, I draped my thigh over his hip, spreading wide for him. I stroked his bearded jaw and stared into his rich, emerald eyes. "Touch me," I whispered.

His thumb brushed that spot between my thighs, and I gasped. Yes, *that* was where I needed him. Ever so slowly he ran another finger along my wet folds, tracing my skin and learning me with exquisite patience. My hips strained toward him, craving more, and I was rewarded by the slow slide of one of his large fingers inside me.

I reached for his trousers again and this time he didn't stop me as I slipped inside and took hold of him. His cock was so thick it barely fit in my hand, and was the perfect mix of velvety soft and rock hard. I couldn't wait to feel it inside me, but for now I was content to wrap my fingers around its length. Slade groaned as I took him in hand and seemed to get even harder somehow. The sound, deep in his throat and all male, only made me desire him even more.

I began stroking his length the way Jasin had showed me, and was rewarded with another low rumbling from

Slade. He slipped a second finger inside me, while his thumb began to rub that spot Auric had once called a clit.

Slade started up a slow rhythm that felt divine and fondled my breasts with his other hand as he claimed my mouth again. While we shared deep, passionate kisses, our fingers began to move faster, bringing us both closer to release. We moaned and sighed as we touched each other, our hips rocking together while my breasts crushed against his broad chest. His thumb pressed harder against my most sensitive spot, and I gasped into his mouth as sensations crashed over me. My body tightened up around his hand as pleasure took hold of me, and then I felt him surge in my palm as he joined me. He kissed me the entire time while the last tremors ran through us both and a sense of satisfaction settled over me.

As our heartbeats slowed to a normal pace, Slade wrapped me in his dark, muscular arms and pulled me against his chest. I snuggled up against him, savoring this closeness and how right it felt. I no longer had to wonder if Slade wanted me or cared for me—he'd showed me the depths of his feelings tonight.

"Thank you," he said, pressing a soft kiss to my forehead. "It's been a long time since I touched another woman that way. I was worried I'd forgotten how."

"You definitely don't need to worry about that," I said with a smile.

"I'm glad to hear it." He slipped his fingers through the long strands of my hair, idly playing with it. "We have a few days while the Resistance prepares and moves into position. I thought perhaps we might visit my village in that time to make sure my family is safe."

I sat up a little to look him in the eyes. "Truly? You're all right with me meeting them?"

"Yes. I think it's time." He cupped my cheek and brought his lips to mine again. "You're my future, Kira. I'm not going to deny that any longer. And it's time everyone knew it too."

16

REVEN

When I woke the next morning, I found the Resistance base a frenzy of activity. Soldiers were arming themselves and preparing for travel, while other people rushed around, delivering supplies and messages, or gathering their things. It would take a week for them to reach Salt Creek Tower since they didn't have dragons they could ride to get their people into position quickly. Those who wouldn't fight would remain here in relative safety, but were prepared to escape if things went badly and the Dragons tracked the Resistance back to Slateden.

I avoided the commotion and found a quiet room used for training that now sat empty, where I pulled out my twin swords. When something was bothering me I found physical exertion and the familiar slice of my blades helped clear my mind. Not that something was bothering me, not exactly. It just annoyed me that I hadn't seen Kira much in the last few days, except when we were in meetings with Parin. She spent all her free time with her other mates, the ones who followed her around like they couldn't stand to be apart from her for a single minute and proclaimed their love daily. I would never be one of those men, and I had no right to demand her time when I couldn't give her anything in return. I shouldn't be annoyed. I shouldn't want her attention all to myself. But I was a selfish bastard at the best of times.

"There you are," Kira said, from the doorway. "For a while there I'd worried you'd run off again."

"I haven't, but I can still change my mind." The reminder of how I'd left her once stung, but I ignored it as I lowered my blades. She wore her hunting leathers today, and I admired the way they clung to her body and showed off her shapely hips and ample breasts. She'd come looking for me, and that was something at least.

"I came to tell you that we're leaving today to visit Slade's village and check that his family is safe. I'd like it if you would come with us, but it's your decision of course."

"I might." If she wanted me there I would go, but I didn't want to seem too eager either. I raised one of my swords. "Care to join me for a couple rounds?"

She stepped into the room, her eyes bright. "I think I can spare a few moments."

I passed her one of my swords, since hers was absent. "How generous of you."

She swung the blade, growing accustomed to its weight. "Don't tell me you missed me."

If only she knew. I gave her a wicked smile. "I'm sure you wish I did."

We each took position across from each other and got into fighting stances. I'd been training with Kira whenever we had a spare moment, usually when we camped for the night or before we took off in the morning, and her form had improved a lot over the last few weeks. She'd never be as good as me (then again, who was?), but I was satisfied she could defend herself better now.

Kira attacked first, but I easily parried her blow and countered with my own. She danced out of the way, and I admired how light on her feet she was. Her eyes took on that determined look I'd seen a lot lately, and she adjusted her stance and struck again.

"You're getting better," I said, as I sidestepped her strike.

"All thanks to you." She gave me a wry grin. "Or should I say thanks to the Black Hood?"

I shook my head at that ridiculous name. "No one calls me that anymore. And I'm happy to take the credit, but you're also more focused these days."

Her grin faded and she gripped the sword tighter. "If I'm going to stop the Dragons, I need to be focused." We traded blows again for some time, before she asked, "What do you think of the plan?"

"It's risky. It assumes the Dragons will leave the Earth Temple to defend against an attack, but there are a lot of things that could go wrong. And you'll be in the center of the danger if it does."

"Then it's a good thing I'll have you with me to watch my back."

That was something I'd insisted on before agreeing to this mad scheme. The plan had Kira and Slade sneaking into the Earth Temple, and there was nothing stealthy about Slade. They needed me to scout ahead and keep them safe. But even if we succeeded, that was only the beginning of our problems.

"And what will we do when it's time to visit the Water Temple?" I asked. "The Dragons won't fall for this trick twice."

Her brows pinched together. "I don't know, but we'll have to worry about that when the time comes."

She attacked me with renewed vigor that I sensed was born out of her own frustration and grief. I decided to let her gain the advantage to boost her confidence, but she struck harder than I expected. The blade flew out of my hand, and a victorious smile lit up her face.

She levelled her sword at my neck. "Surrender."

"Never." We were both breathing heavily from the exertion, and the air became thick with sexual tension. I darted forward and stole the sword from her hand, then pressed her back against the wall, the blade at her throat. "You still have a lot to learn."

She gazed into my eyes as I pinned her there, and I became aware of the rise and fall of her breasts and the feel of her soft body against me. "I'm eager to learn anything you want to teach me."

Her words brought all sorts of naughty things to mind, and I couldn't resist capturing her lips with mine. The sword fell from my hand and hit the ground with a sharp clang, but I was too wrapped up in kissing Kira to care. I caged her in, then dragged her arms up over her head, pinning them to the wall. With one hand I held her there, as I let my other hand skim down her side, finally allowing myself to touch her the way I wanted. Last time she'd initiated the kiss, but now it was my turn.

Her body melded against mine as the kiss grew deeper and more intense. When my thumb slid over her taut nipple it earned me a soft, delicious gasp. Her touch, her taste, her responsiveness...it all made me want to devour her.

"Kira, are you in here?" Brin's voice called. I jerked away from Kira and released her arms as the door to the room opened. Brin poked her head in, then flashed a knowing grin. "Sorry, didn't mean to interrupt."

I reached down and picked up both my swords, then sheathed them. "It's fine. We were done anyway."

Brin nodded. "We're almost ready to get going."

"I'll be right there," Kira said.

Brin shut the door and left us alone again. I turned back to Kira, who stared at me, her face flushed, her lips parted. I immediately wanted to haul her against me and take her mouth again, but that moment had passed.

"Will you join us?" Kira asked.

I had no interest in meeting Slade's family or visiting another small, boring village, but the thought of being apart from Kira suddenly seemed unbearable. If it were any other woman I would have walked away by now, but for some reason I couldn't stay away from her. "I will, but only because someone needs to be there to keep you all out of danger."

"Of course." She granted me another smile that tempted me to reach for her again, and I forced myself to turn away. Curse this stupid destiny that tied me to her. It would make fools of both of us before the end. Especially when she realized I would never be able to love her the way she wanted.

17

KIRA

Slade's village, Clayridge, was to the west of the Resistance hideout, and as we flew toward it, anxious butterflies flittered around my stomach at the thought of meeting his family. I'd already met both Jasin and Auric's parents, but for some reason this visit made me the most nervous. Maybe because I sensed how close Slade was with his family and I desperately wanted them to accept me. I worried too that the Dragons had found out who Slade was and done the same thing to Clayridge as they did to Stoneham. I could only pray that his family remained anonymous and safe.

Jasin and Auric flew high, their wings brushing the clouds, to avoid us being detected. Parin's words made us cautious, knowing that rumors were already beginning about us—rumors that could bring the Dragons after more innocent people if we weren't careful.

When we flew over Clayridge and saw it was still intact, I let out a sigh of relief. From where he sat behind me, Slade gave me a slight squeeze of his arms. His family was still safe from the Dragons—now I just needed to get them to like me.

My dragons discreetly set down in the nearby forest and returned to their human forms, and then we walked toward the town. Clayridge was about the same size as Stoneham, but it was set up on a hill with a river flowing down below. The terrain was especially rocky, but Slade led us along a well-trodden path up toward the village. Red clay roofs began to appear as we crested the hill, and soon I could see a cluster of stone buildings with a thick wall between them and us. A wall that was meant to protect against elemental attacks, dotted with braziers that could be lit at any moment and large buckets likely filled with water.

A lookout guard stood on top of the wall near the gate, and called out to us as we approached. "Slade, that you?"

Slade chuckled softly. "It's me, Lon. Let us in, will you?"

"Aye!" the young guard called out, then disappeared from view. The gate slowly creaked open moments later, and we were quickly surrounded by cheery dark-skinned men and women who all wanted to welcome Slade back to the village. He greeted each of them with a kind word, a pat on the back, or a warm nod as he led us inside. My nerves wound even tighter as I smiled at everyone, who would no doubt know who we all were by the end of the night. In a small town like this, nothing remained a secret for very long.

As we moved inside the village, more people came out of

the houses and shops to give Slade a wave and a fond greeting. Everyone seemed to know him and love him here, and with each step some of his hard demeanor melted away. It made me wonder what he was like before he'd been sent to find me against his will. Or before Faya had broken his heart.

Ahead of us, an older, sturdy woman with warm brown eyes rushed out of a small house. "Slade! You've returned!"

"Mother," Slade said, as a smile lit up his face. An actual smile. Had I ever seen him truly smile before? Not like this, certainly.

The two of them collided in a tight embrace, and then she pulled back and took his face in her hands. "Oh, I'm so glad you're safe. Let me look at you." She patted his cheeks like he was a boy, even though he towered over her. "We were all so worried after you left. Are you all right?"

"I'm fine." He turned toward us as if to begin introductions, but was interrupted by another woman leaping out of the house and running toward him.

"Big brother!" the young woman cried out. She was about my age and strikingly beautiful, with smooth dark skin and braids piled atop her head. Like Slade, she was tall, but she had also the curves of her mother. I remembered Slade mentioning his younger sister was a troublemaker, and I suspected part of it was because of the way she looked—she would always turn heads.

"Leni!" Slade laughed as he swept his sister up in his arms and twirled her around.

More people streamed toward us, enveloping Slade and giving him warm hugs and kisses on his cheek. I sensed family resemblance in most of them, and a sense of longing spread through me as I watched awkwardly from the sidelines with Brin and my other mates. We were outsiders, forced to watch the celebration, and it was a keen reminder that I didn't have a family anymore. And even when I had one, it had been nothing like this.

Jasin glanced at the others and cleared his throat, before speaking to me. "I think we'll go find an inn and get some rooms while you meet the family."

I started to protest, but then saw how tight Jasin's face was and remembered how he'd been upset around Auric's family too. His own parents had betrayed us not long ago, and seeing this probably reminded him of what he'd lost. Explaining the situation to Slade's family would be easier without my other mates at my side too.

I gave Jasin's arm a quick squeeze. "All right. I'll find you later."

The four of them slipped away, leaving me alone to face the crowd. I swallowed hard and plastered on a smile, unsure of what else I should do.

Eventually Slade was able to break apart from his family. He moved to my side and took my hand in his, sending a signal to all of them that we were close. Warm happiness filled me, even as color spread to my cheeks. "Everyone, this is Kira. She's the one I was sent to find by the Earth God."

"Kira, welcome to Clayridge," Slade's mother said, as she moved forward to embrace me in a warm hug. "I'm Yena, Slade's mother."

"It's so nice to meet you," I said.

Slade brought two women over to me—the curvy sister I'd seen before, and another one who was a little more plain but had the same striking green eyes as Slade. "These are my sisters, Leni and Wrin."

"Hello—" I started to reply, but Slade was already continuing his introductions.

"And this is Wrin's husband Merl, and their son Tam," he said, indicating a lighter-skinned man and a boy I guessed to be about five. Slade then pointed to more people surrounding us. "I'd also like you to meet my aunt Edda, my uncle Heim, and their son Noren, who took over as the town's blacksmith for me."

I quickly nodded at a woman who looked a lot like Yena but taller and thinner, an older bearded man, and a young man who had Slade's muscles and gave me a kind smile. Slade then went on to introduce me to a dozen other cousins, distant relations, and friends of the family who had joined us—so many I knew I would never remember anyone's names. They all gave me hugs or shook my hands, and it was both overwhelming and wonderful. With so much love it was no wonder Slade had never wanted to leave this place.

"Get back, let the poor girl have some room to breathe," Yena said, as she forced her way through the crowd to me.

She interlocked our arms and began to lead me toward the small house I assumed was her own. "Come now. We must have dinner, and then you can tell us everything about yourself."

Everything? I swallowed hard as the nervous butterflies returned to my stomach. Now the interrogation would begin.

18

KIRA

Yena led us inside her home, which was cozy and warm with a stone hearth already lit. Slade spoke a few more words to the people outside before following us, along with his sister Leni. We were immediately swept into the dining area, with a long wooden table and two benches. The air smelled of freshly baked treats.

"Sit down and relax," Yena said, as she nudged me to the bench. "You must be exhausted after all your travels. I'll get us some food and you can tell me all about your journeys."

"That's very kind of you." I slid onto the bench and Slade moved in beside me.

"Be careful, or mother will stuff you so full of food you'll never be able to walk again," Leni said, as she sat across from me. She gave me a warm, dazzling smile that reminded me so much of Tash it sent a pang of longing and grief through my heart.

The door banged open and Slade's other sister Wrin came inside too. "You better not start without me."

"Of course not, dear," Yena said. "We'd love for you to join us. Where are Merl and Tam?"

Wrin sat beside her sister. "I sent them home for the night. They weren't happy about it, but I'm not missing out on hearing what Slade's been doing all this time."

"I'm sure it will be all over town by the morning anyway," Leni said, rolling her eyes.

Wrin studied me with intelligent, serious eyes that looked so much like Slade's. "So you're the woman he left Clayridge to go find."

I ducked my head. "I am, yes. Although I didn't ask for any of this either."

Slade's mother began dropping wooden bowls of steaming hot stew in front of each of us. Wrin jumped up and brought over a loaf of bread, while Leni served everyone some ale. Everything about it reminded me of my time with Tash and her family in Stoneham, from the delicious smell of the stew to the slightly bitter taste of the ale. Grief tried to sink its claws in me again, but I forced it back down. Stoneham and Tash were gone, but Clayridge and Slade's family were alive, and I would do everything in my power to keep it that way.

When all the food was served, Yena plopped down across from us. "Eat! No need to wait for me."

Slade wasted no time digging in and then he closed his

eyes as he savored the stew. "It's been far too long since I had good food like this."

Yena smiled and patted her son's hand. "There's nothing better than a home cooked meal. Now eat up, you're looking far too skinny after all that travel."

I held in a laugh. Slade looked anything but skinny. He was a mountain of a man made of pure muscle with arms the size of tree trunks, but I sensed this was just Yena's way.

She gave me a smile. "You too dear. You're very pretty, but you could use some more meat on those bones of yours."

I flushed and shoveled a spoonful of stew into my mouth. Warm flavors exploded on my lips, and I caught the taste of rabbit, carrots, and more. It was definitely better than the food we'd been eating while on the road. "Thank you. It's delicious."

"Glad you like it." She barely touched her own food and instead took in the both of us while we ate, like she couldn't drink in enough of us with her eyes to satisfy her.

Leni pointed her spoon at Slade. "You better start talking, or mother is going to burst with impatience."

"Let them swallow their food at least," Wrin said, shaking her head.

Slade slowed down, his bowl already half empty, and glanced at me. I had no idea how much these women knew already and I was completely overwhelmed by the situation, but I sensed he wanted me to speak. I set down my spoon and asked, "What did Slade tell you before he left?"

"We knew that the Earth God had chosen him for a great mission," Yena said, her voice bursting with pride. "He was given great powers, and then was sent to find and protect you...although he was unable to tell us why."

"None of us believed it at first, until he showed us his magic," Wrin said.

I arched an eyebrow at Slade. "I thought you weren't supposed to tell anyone about your encounter with the Earth God."

Slade shrugged. "You try keeping a secret from these three."

"He had to tell us something, or no one would have let him leave Clayridge," Leni said.

Wrin nodded. "It's true, my brother is a very important and respected member of this village. He could have been the next mayor, if he'd wanted."

Slade scowled and shook his head. "I was a simple blacksmith, nothing more."

"Nonsense, dear," Yena said, before turning to me. "Slade worked hard to keep this town running and make sure it was safe. Beyond what he did as blacksmith, he volunteered with the town guard and convinced everyone to build the outer wall after an elemental attack took two lives. We've been attacked three more times since then, but we've always held them off thanks to Slade."

"Three?" Slade asked, his spoon pausing halfway to his mouth. "There was another one while I was gone?"

"Yes, this time an air elemental, if you can believe that. Must have wandered far from the Air Realm to make it all the way out here." Yena shrugged. "We were able to keep it out without any issue."

"Good to hear," Slade said, though I could tell it bothered him that he hadn't been here to protect his town. He obviously cared a great deal for the people of Clayridge.

"Now hurry up and tell us where you've been all this time," Leni said.

The others gave Slade expectant looks, and he finally sighed and launched into the tale of how the Earth God had chosen him as the new Jade Dragon, how he'd found me along with my other mates, and how we were on a quest to overthrow the Black Dragon and had recently joined up with the Resistance to help us get into the Earth Temple. I stayed quiet as I ate my stew, worried about what his family would think of all this—especially Slade sharing me with three other men.

"That's quite a tale," Yena said, when Slade lapsed into silence. "And it all sounds quite dangerous, but I'm sure the Earth God chose you because he knew you could handle it all. I'm very proud of you, Slade."

"It sounds incredible," Leni said, her eyes dancing with excitement. "I wish I could have been there for all of it."

"You're not upset about me being only one of her mates?" Slade asked.

"It's not something I'm comfortable with myself," Yena

said slowly, as she glanced at me. "But who are we to questions the Gods?"

Wrin nodded. "You can't turn your back on the Earth God's will. Do you think you'll get to speak to him at the temple?"

"I expect so," Slade said.

A knock sounded on the door and Yena got up to open it. Brin stood on the other side and was quickly ushered in. "You're one of Slade and Kira's companions aren't you?" Yena asked. "You must join us!"

"Thank you," Brin said with a smile as she stepped inside. Her eyes caught sight of Leni and her gaze seemed to linger there before she turned to me. "I simply wanted to let Kira know that we've booked rooms at the inn for the next few nights."

"Very good," Yena said. "I'd love to house you all, but as you can see my home is rather small. But please, sit with us and I'll get you some food. And tell us your name, child."

Brin hesitated, but then slid beside me. Across from Leni, who was definitely watching my friend with interest. "My name is Brin of House Pashona, and it's an honor to join you for a meal."

"House Pashona?" Leni asked, even more intrigued. She leaned forward, giving us a glimpse of her ample cleavage. "You're nobility?"

Brin offered her an alluring smile. "I am, yes. From the Air Realm. But please, don't let that change your opinion of me. As you can see, I'm simply one of Kira's traveling companions now."

"Brin is a good friend," I said. "I'm lucky she agreed to join us. Being with four men all the time can get rather... complicated. It's nice to have a woman I can talk with."

Leni let out a dramatic sigh and rested her chin on her hand. "You're all so lucky, traveling the world, fighting bandits and Dragons, helping the Resistance. I'd do anything to get out of this boring town."

"Why don't you?" Brin asked.

"Definitely not," Slade said. "She's too young."

"I'm twenty-one!" Leni said, then turned to me and Brin. "How old are you two?"

"Twenty," I replied, while Brin said, "Twenty-two."

"See, they're the same age as me," Leni said. "And Slade, you started helping the Resistance at my age. Why am I not allowed to do anything?"

Yena returned and set a bowl in front of Brin, then patted Leni's head like a child. "It's not safe for you. Slade had to leave to fulfill his destiny, but your place is here."

"My place is wherever I decide it is," Leni said, as she rose to her feet. "And I don't plan on staying in Clayridge for the rest of my life."

She walked out of the house, while her mother sighed. "I'm sorry for that. She's been like this ever since Slade left."

"I'll talk to her," Slade said.

"She'll get over it," Wrin said. "Just like she got over that traveling merchant who stopped by. And the soldier before that."

"Leni has always had her head full of big dreams. I'm not sure she'll ever be satisfied here." Yena waved it away with a sad smile. "But enough of that. Tell us more about you, Kira. Where are you from?"

I took a deep breath and settled in to tell them about my life. I could already tell this was going to be a long night.

19

AURIC

W hile Kira spent time with Slade's family, the rest of us took over most of the inn. Brin grew restless and went off to explore the town on her own, while Reven, Jasin, and I shared a meal together. Jasin and I both ate like we had the hunger of five men after flying for much of the day, while Reven watched with amusement. We'd been served some sort of questionable stew common in the Earth Realm, a far cry from the fine dining of the Air Realm, but I was so hungry I didn't care. And maybe I'd gotten used to such things after weeks of travel, because it actually tasted pretty good.

"Kira has an idea for how we can increase our bond," Jasin said, in between bites. "If she returns tonight, we should meet for more...training."

I arched an eyebrow. "Sounds promising."

"Is that what you two call it?" Reven asked. "Training?"

"Jasin has been very instructive," I said.

Reven snickered. "I'll bet he has."

"You're welcome to join us too," Jasin said. "I'm sure Kira would enjoy that."

Reven paused as he brought his tankard of ale to his lips. "Perhaps some other time."

We retreated to our rooms after our meal. I'd splurged and gotten everyone their own rooms since the inn was empty and my father had given us plenty of gold for our journey. But as soon as I was alone in mine, a creeping loneliness settled over me. I'd spent the last few weeks sharing a tent with Jasin, and I found myself missing his presence. Who would have thought the two of us would become so close, when we'd originally hated each other?

I debated going to his room, but dismissed the thought as too childish. What would we even talk about? Jasin was a former soldier, and I was a former prince. We had little in common besides Kira. It was incredible we managed to get along at all.

I decided to open my notebook and add some notes about our journey while I waited. I'd recorded everything we'd been through so far in the hopes it would be of use someday, perhaps to our daughter when it was her turn to become the next Black Dragon. Assuming we didn't fail— but I refused to entertain that thought.

When a knock sounded on my door an hour later, I rushed to open it. Jasin and Kira stood on the other side, and my heart pounded with anticipation.

"How was your evening with Slade's family?" I asked, as they stepped inside my dimly-lit room.

"Good." Kira sat on the edge of the bed. "Better than I expected, although it was a little overwhelming. I'm glad I got to meet his family though." She rubbed the spot on the bed next to her. "But I'm happy to have some time away from them too. Did Jasin explain the plan?"

I sank onto the bed beside her. "Not in any detail."

"She thinks the key to strengthening our bond is to share her body together," Jasin said with a grin. He took the spot on the other side of Kira and began slowly massaging her shoulders.

I grinned back at him. "I like the sound of that."

"We thought you might," Kira said, as she leaned into Jasin's touch. He slid his hands down her arms and began to kiss her neck, making her sigh. I watched them for a few moments, enjoying the sight of Jasin bringing my mate pleasure, but then I couldn't resist joining in.

I took her mouth in a hungry kiss and cupped her breasts in my palms, teasing her hard nipples through the fabric of her dress. It had been a week since we'd bonded at the Air Temple, and I was eager to be inside her again. But even once we'd done this a thousand times, I knew I'd never get enough of her. She was my one and only—my mate.

Jasin and I both gripped the fabric of Kira's dress and worked it up, pulling it above her head and tossing it aside. Once she was completely nude I let my eyes soak her in, devouring the sight of her bare skin and lush curves. Gods, I could stare at this woman forever.

The door creaked open behind me, and we all froze. I snapped out of it and quickly moved in front of Kira to block her from sight. The three of us turned as one to look at the door—and saw Reven standing there.

20

KIRA

R even paused in the doorway, his eyes slowly taking in the scene. "Apologies. I thought this was my room."

From the tone of his voice, I didn't believe that for a second—but I didn't mind either. If anything, the thought that he'd come to join us only made my already racing heart pound even faster.

"Don't go," I said.

He lingered at the door, perhaps waiting for someone to protest or taking a moment to make up his mind. Or maybe he wanted even more of an invitation.

I reached toward him. "Join us."

That finally brought him forward. He shut the door, his eyes never leaving the scene before him of my naked body pressed between Jasin and Auric. "I'll stay...but just to watch."

Reven crossed the room and sank into an armchair in the corner, his pose deceptively casual, and laced his arms behind his head as if waiting for the show to begin. Desire flared between my thighs at the thought of his piercing blue gaze on me the entire time I was making love to the other men.

But I couldn't forget Auric and Jasin either. I wanted them to be comfortable with this. I touched both of their chests, glancing between them. "Are you all right with this?" I asked in a low voice.

Auric threaded his fingers through mine. "I want whatever makes you happy."

Jasin's lips touched my ear. "I invited him earlier. I didn't think he would actually come though."

"You did?" I asked.

A naughty grin touched his lips. "I thought you would like it."

"You know me so well," I said, before catching that grin in a passionate kiss. Not long ago I'd been a virgin. Now the thought of multiple men touching me at the same time seemed not only natural, but right. I blamed Jasin for corrupting me, although it was Auric who'd first initiated these training sessions. Maybe he was to blame too. Not that I minded one bit.

The two men surrounding me resumed their kissing and touching, as if we'd never been interrupted and didn't have another man watching our every move. I helped remove their clothes, sliding my hands along their smooth, hard bodies that I loved so much. They were both so perfect, sometimes it was hard to believe they were mine.

"Tonight we're going to try something new as part of your training," Jasin said, as his hand slipped between my thighs, finding me already wet. But then his fingers slid back, back, back, to my other, forbidden entrance. "I'm going to take you here tonight, while Auric takes you from the front."

My eyes widened. He'd talked about claiming me from behind before, and the idea had intrigued me—especially if it meant joining with both of them at the same time. "Will it hurt?"

"A little, but it will feel good too." He nibbled on my ear. "Trust me."

I closed my eyes and relaxed against him. "I do."

With his other hand, he reached for a vial of liquid from the nightstand. "I got this in the Air Realm. The oil will make it easier, and we'll go slow. If it's too much, we'll stop."

I nodded, eager to get started, even though I was nervous too. While Auric began slowly stroking me between my legs, Jasin coated his fingers in oil and began to work it into me from behind. I gasped at the sensation, though it didn't hurt, not at all. When Auric's fingers entered me in front too, I got a glimpse of what the rest of the night would be like...and I wanted more. I bore down against their hands, taking them deeper, and Auric's mouth found mine again. While the two of them stretched me out and moved inside me, my tongue slid against Auric's in a sensual dance. Jasin kissed the back of my neck, and everything felt so good I wasn't sure how it could ever get better...but knew this was just the beginning.

"Good," Jasin said. "You're ready. Now sit on Auric, but don't take him inside you yet."

Auric gathered me into his arms and I climbed onto his lap, straddling his hips, his cock brushing up against me. I took his length in hand and began to stroke it, while leaning forward to kiss him some more. His hands found my breasts and he began caressing my nipples, while I felt Jasin's cock brush against me from behind. I tensed up, but he kissed my shoulder and whispered, "Relax."

His warm voice calmed me, and my body became pliant at his touch. He began to push inside my back entrance, and at first the stretching was so intense it took my breath away. He already felt huge, and it seemed impossible he'd be able to fit completely inside, but he kept going. Gods, it was so tight, I wasn't sure I could stand it. My fingers dug into Auric's shoulders and Jasin paused.

"You're doing great," Jasin said, kissing my neck some more. "Almost there."

"Keep going," I said, as I willed my body to relax. "I want this."

Auric's fingers found my clit while I continued stroking him, and when he began to rub me there it all got so much easier. The sensations were so intense, and I found myself pushing back against Jasin, wanting more. The pain vanished, until only pleasure remained.

When he was fully sheathed, we both let out a delirious

sigh. Jasin felt huge inside me, but still it wasn't enough. I needed Auric too.

Without words, Jasin and Auric shared a look that communicated everything that had to be done. Jasin's fingers dug into my hips as he lifted me slightly, while Auric guided himself into me. I sank down onto his hard cock, taking him deep inside, and if I'd thought it was a tight fit before, it was nothing compared to having both of them inside me. As my hips rested against Auric's, I closed my eyes and savored the exquisite fullness with both of them inside me, their bodies pressed tight against me on all sides.

"Still all right?" Jasin asked.

"It's amazing," I said, breathless. I turned my head and drew Jasin in for a kiss, then brought Auric close for one too. Their mouths both pressed against my lips, their tongues sliding into me, and I found myself kissing them both at the same time. The kiss deepened, the three of our lips and tongues tangling together in the most intimate way. Soon I had no idea where I ended or any of them began. We'd truly all become one.

Our kiss broke apart as we became overwhelmed with the need to move. Jasin began, slowly pulling out of me before sliding back in. The tightness back there made me gasp, but my body quickly grew used to it, and then Auric began lifting his hips to thrust into me too. I clung to his body, unable to do anything but take what they were giving me and enjoy every second of it.

I could tell they were overcome by it too, from the way

they groaned against me and bucked harder. And when Jasin reached out and grasped Auric's muscular arm, it nearly became too much for me. Especially when I felt Auric's hand slide from my naked hip to Jasin's, urging him on. It wasn't just me with them, it was all three of us bonding together and sharing this moment.

I raised my head and my eyes locked with Reven, who stared at the scene with rapt attention. I wanted to give him a show. I wanted him to see what he could have too, some-day. If only he would let me in.

But then he stood and came toward the bed, surprising me. He bent down, took my chin in his hand, and captured my lips in a kiss. I reached for him, my fingers sliding around his neck, but then he pulled back and straightened up. But I didn't want to let him go.

I gripped his shirt, then slid my hand down to his trousers, pressing against the hardness there. He'd defi-nitely enjoyed watching, and that knowledge only made me more excited. I tore at his trousers, yanking them open, revealing his long length. He didn't stop me. Instead, he gazed down at me with his intense blue eyes as I took his cock in hand and brought it to my lips. My mouth slid over the head and he let out a soft groan, while tangling his fingers in my hair.

Auric and Jasin kept going through it all, rocking me between their bodies, their pace growing faster. I couldn't hold on much longer, not with the incredible feelings they sent through me. But I needed Reven too, that was clear to me now. It couldn't be just me with Auric and Jasin forever, I needed *all* of my mates equally.

I took Reven into my mouth as far as I could, while circling the base of his shaft with my hand. He gripped my hair tighter and his hips jerked, like he couldn't help himself. Like he didn't want to give himself to me, but was unable to resist.

I sucked on him hard, feeling my own release approach. I sensed through the bond that Auric and Jasin were close too, but they were holding out for me. Together the four of us moved in a sensual dance, back and forth, in and out, with my body taking everything they gave me and still wanting more. If only Slade were here too...

The instant Reven reached down to pinch my nipple, I was gone. His touch pushed me over the edge, and I cried out while tightening up around Auric and Jasin. Ripples of pleasure more intense than anything I'd ever felt before began to overwhelm me, and I was completely lost in the sensations. They were my mates, and in this moment I truly felt as though I belonged to all of them.

Each man released himself into me only seconds later, while I was still trembling. Jasin's head pressed against my neck as he came hard into my behind, while Auric thrust up into me faster until his seed filled me. Reven was last, gripping my hair tight while he finally let himself go into my mouth. I swallowed everything he gave me and our eyes remained locked on each other's, though his face was indecipherable.

When it was done, he slipped out of me, closed up his trousers, and then walked out of the room without a word. It was just like him, and all I could do was sigh and shake my head, while relaxing against my other two mates.

We fell onto the bed, the three of us a tangle of bodies without end. The kissing began again, hands sliding against each other's skin, this time to comfort and show affection rather than induce desire or pleasure. The bond between us felt stronger than ever, and I sensed their satisfaction and love through it. Not just for me, but for each other too. It amazed me how far they'd come from those first jealous fights and heated arguments to snuggling together on the bed, with me pressed between their naked bodies. I loved them both so much, and nothing made me happier than knowing they'd truly come to care about the other during the last few months. Well, except for the thought of my other two mates joining me in bed like this too.

Someday, maybe...I could hope.

2 1

KIRA

In the morning Slade showed me around the small village, pointing out the houses of friends and relatives, or showing me things he had helped repair. A lot of it reminded me of Stoneham, although Clayridge was better defended—not that it would have helped against the Dragons anyway.

The tour ended at a stone house near his mother's, with smoke coming out of the chimney. "This used to be my house and my shop," Slade said. "But now my cousin Noren lives here."

"You said he took over as the town's blacksmith?" I asked.

"Yes. Before that he was my apprentice. I would have liked to train him for a few more years, but the Gods had other plans."

He led me around the back of the house, where the shop

was located. There was a gray horse tied to a post nearby, and a wave of heat struck me as we approached the open door. Inside, Noren stood over an anvil, where he was working on a horseshoe. A large stone forge took up one wall, and against the other was a table with a variety of metal tongs and hammers with a sketch of some armor. Over it was a shelf with some helmets and gauntlets, while a variety of weapons and shields hung from the walls.

Noren looked up and brushed sweat off his forehead. "Morning."

"I came to see how you're holding up," Slade said.

"Meaning you want to see if I'm keeping up the family legacy." Noren grinned. "It wasn't easy at first, but I managed without you. I've taken on my own apprentice now too."

Slade clasped him on the shoulder. "Good man."

They chatted a bit longer about blacksmith things I didn't understand, before we stepped outside again. I gave the horse a quick rub, and then Slade and I kept walking, taking a leisurely stroll down the hill to the river and the surrounding forest.

"Do you feel better now that you know the shop is in good hands?" I asked.

"A little," Slade said. "Although Noren seems so young to me. Too young to be running the shop. Then again, I was his age when I took over for my father too."

I guessed Noren was about my age, and it hit me how much older and more experienced Slade was. He'd talked about how he'd been settled in his life, and for the first time I truly understood what he'd meant. He'd spent years building his profession and helping his town, and then he'd been forced to give all of that up. For me.

"How old are you?" I asked Slade, realizing I didn't know the exact number.

"Thirty-two."

I missed a step in my surprise. Twelve years older than me. "Truly?"

He reached out to steady me with a hand on my elbow. "Too old for you?"

"No, not at all." I continued walking. "But it's no wonder you think the rest of us young and foolish."

"Young, yes," he said with a trace of amusement. "Foolish...sometimes."

"I can see now why you had a hard time giving up this life."

"It was difficult, but I don't regret it. After Faya left, this town was never the same for me. It wasn't until finding you that I began to feel whole again—like I'd discovered my true place in the world. This village will always be my home, but it's no longer where I belong."

"And where is that?" I asked, as I stopped beside the river.

"By your side." He cupped my cheek in his hand. "Wherever you go, I'll be there with you."

"My loyal protector," I murmured, as I leaned into his touch.

His head lowered and his mouth pressed against mine. He gripped my hip, digging his fingers into the fabric of my dress while he kissed me long and hard until I was practically moaning for more. I slid my hands down his chest and under his shirt, running my fingers across his bare stomach.

A sharp sound in the forest broke us apart, and I was reminded of when Cadock's bandits had interrupted us before. But as I peered through the trees it wasn't bandits I saw, but two young women raising swords at each other. Leni and Brin lunged and parried, laughing as they danced away from each other and then drew close again. There was something about the way they moved and looked at each other that made it clear this was more than just sword fighting practice.

"You're better than I expected," Brin said, her voice carrying through the leaves. "Where did you learn to fight?"

"Slade and Noren taught me," Leni said, as their swords clashed again. "I joined the town guard three years ago, and became its leader when Slade left to find Kira. What about you?"

"My parents had me trained in combat from the time I could hold a sword. They were terribly worried their precious only child would be kidnapped and held for ransom or some such. It's never happened, of course, but I can hardly complain."

"Impressive. I'll admit, you might be able to teach me a thing or two."

"Oh, I can teach you a great many things, my dear," Brin said, her voice sensual.

I covered my mouth to hide my amusement, especially since their conversation so closely mirrored the one I'd had with Reven the other day. I had a feeling theirs would end the same way too.

"One of them is going to get hurt," Slade said, shaking his head.

"Brin is an expert swordswoman, and your sister doesn't seem too bad either."

"Not what I meant." He scowled as he watched them tumble to the ground together, their laughter ringing out around us.

I took his hand and led him away from what was likely to become an intimate moment. "Let them have their few moments of happiness. They're fleeting enough at the moment."

He let me drag him away, and then entwined his fingers with mine. Just the simple act of holding hands with him was so much more than I ever thought I would get from him, and I took my own advice and allowed myself to feel content.

"You seem happier too," he said, studying my face. "After Stoneham we were all worried about you."

"I'm still upset about that, and I'll miss Tash forever, but coming here and meeting your family has eased some of the pain." I squeezed his hand. "Thank you for bringing us here.

You seem like a weight has been lifted off your shoulders too."

Slade nodded. "Once my family knew the truth about our situation, it became easier for me to accept as well."

"That's a relief. I worried after what happened with Faya you would never be okay with it."

He spoke slowly as we continued back along the river toward the village. "It was different with Faya. I never believed she loved both me and Parin. As soon as she was forced to choose between us, she picked him and abandoned the life we'd created together without a second thought. That's why I couldn't understand how you would be able to love all of us equally, but now I know you're nothing like her. She went behind my back and cheated on me. You've been up front about this complicated relationship with me from the beginning, and you've never tried to hide anything about it. That honesty is important."

"Does that mean you're not upset about having to share me with the others anymore?"

"I don't mind it as much as I used to," Slade admitted. "Traveling the world with you and the others has opened my mind to a lot of things I never experienced while living in Clayridge. I suppose being one of your mates has changed me too. I only want you to be happy, whether it's because of me or the other men. Or all of us."

An image came to mind of Slade joining in while I was being shared between the other three men and I felt a flush of heat between my legs. I doubted Slade would ever want to do that, but I couldn't deny the idea excited me.

As if conjured by my thoughts, Jasin and Auric emerged from the village, heading for the river. We'd agreed to meet in the afternoon to continue our training, but I hadn't realized the day had gotten so late.

"Ready to get started?" Jasin asked, as they approached.

"If we're interrupting, we can come back later," Auric said.

"We're going to try to summon lightning again," I explained to Slade. "Do you mind?"

"No, it's fine. My mother has demanded my help with fixing her roof this afternoon anyway." He lowered his head and brushed a kiss across my lips. "I'll see you tonight for dinner."

"I wouldn't miss it."

He headed back toward the village, and I turned to my two mates with a smile I couldn't hide. They'd both noticed the kiss, judging by the smirks on their faces.

"Things with Slade are better then," Jasin said.

"They are. He's finally starting to open up to me, and he said he's getting used to the idea of sharing me with the rest of you."

"That's good to hear," Auric said. "For a while, I was worried he wouldn't be able to do his duty at the Earth Temple."

"I don't think that will be a problem anymore," I said, my face flushing for no good reason. I'd shared my body with both these men last night, so why did talking about being intimate with Slade feel so embarrassing? Maybe because our budding relationship was more private, and a part of me wanted to keep it that way.

Jasin took my hand in his. "I'm glad you're happy. Now let's get to work."

22

JASIN

As soon as I touched Kira our ever-present bond sparked bright, like a fire suddenly flaring to life. I always felt her in the background of my mind, but her presence became almost overwhelming when we touched.

She reached for Auric with her other hand, connecting the three of us. "Can you sense each other?"

"Yes," Auric said, his eyes closed. "Much stronger than before."

I closed my eyes and reached out, sorting through the tangled threads of identity and emotion to separate Kira, Auric, and myself. I focused on the feeling of Auric and followed the trail back, going deeper than ever before. He was a mix of excitement and nervousness, but I stretched beyond all that until I found his core self. His strength, his wisdom, his innate goodness. And there, wrapped up in all of that, was his air magic.

"I feel it too," I said.

"Now draw upon your magic while reaching for the other one's power," Kira said. "Try to combine the two elements of fire and air to create lightning."

As I seized the magic, I felt both Kira and Auric inside me, tugging and pulling, searching and finding. Fire came to me as if by instinct now, but drawing upon Auric's magic was a lot harder. Every time I tried to grasp it, it seemed to slip through my fingers.

I heard a low buzzing sound and opened my eyes to small sparks flashing in front of us. My hand tightened around Kira's as I tried to build up the magic, but then it fizzled out and was lost. The sparks vanished.

I ran a hand through my hair. "Damn. We almost had it."

"Maybe we just need more time for the bond to grow stronger," Auric suggested.

Kira sighed. "We don't have time. We face the Dragons in only a few days, and we have to be prepared."

"Then we keep trying." I reached out and grabbed Auric's hand too, forming a circle between the three of us. Instead of closing my eyes, I looked straight into Auric's gray ones. And then I reached for the magic again.

A bolt of bright white energy shot down from the sky and hit the tree beside us, making us all jump. The energy disappeared instantly, but left behind the impression of heat and power, along with the blackened remains of a tree trunk.

"We did it," Auric said, his voice impressed.

"Yeah, we did," I said, dropping their hands. "But I'm not sure what good it does us. We can't stand around in a circle holding hands every time we need to call lightning."

"Sark and Isen summoned it at the Air Temple without even touching," Kira said. "We simply need to practice more."

"At least we know it's possible now," Auric said.

Kira held out her hands as she glanced at both of us. "Let's try it again."

I groaned, but took hold of both of them and called forth the magic again. The lightning came easier this time, but it was erratic, hitting the surface of the water with a jagged strike. We were going to have to spend all our free time practicing this to be able to actually control the magic in a way that would be useful in battle. Right now we had just as much of a chance of hitting each other as the enemy.

"Good," Kira said, after the next three attempts. "Now do it again."

"Couldn't we go back to the other kind of training?" I asked, flashing her a naughty grin. "I liked that a lot better."

"We all did," Auric said.

Kira shook her head. "We will at night, and during the day we're going to do this. Every day until you're throwing lightning from your hands like you throw fire and air."

I groaned, but then turned to Auric. "Fine, but let's at least make this more fun. Ten coins says I can throw lightning before you can."

His eyes gleamed as he smirked at me, that old competition between us coming back to the surface, except this time in a friendly way. "You're on."

23

KIRA

Over the next few days we settled into a slower pace while staying in Clayridge that seemed to suit all of us. I practiced sword fighting with Reven, trained in magic with Auric and Jasin, and spent time with Slade and his family. After such a long time on the road, it was good for all of us to stop and breathe for a while. News had spread through the village about what we were, and people treated us with respect and awe, but otherwise little changed. Meanwhile, Brin and Leni got even closer—I caught sight of them kissing numerous times, and while their relationship seemed destined for heartbreak, none of us wanted to interfere with their happiness. But we all knew how hard it would be when it came time for us to leave.

We only had a few more days until we were supposed to meet the Resistance at the Earth Temple and I keenly felt our time running out with each minute. Once we left

Clayridge we would have to face the Dragons again, and there was no guarantee any of us would survive the encounter. I pushed myself to train even harder, remembering Tash's blackened bones and the ruins of my village.

It was while training with Jasin and Auric by the river that we heard a panicked shout ring out in town. We immediately stopped what we were doing and rushed back into the village, searching for the source of the trouble.

Brin rushed over to us as soon as we stepped through the gate. "One of the Dragons has been spotted heading this way!"

Jasin let out a growl. "Auric and I can take him."

I shook my head, my heart clenching. "No, you'll put the people here in danger. The Dragons can't know we've been here."

"Do we have time to escape?" Auric asked.

"I don't think so," Brin said. "We have to find somewhere for you to hide."

"My old house," Slade said, from behind us. "I used to hide Resistance members in a panel in the floor."

Reven stepped out of the shadows. "How do you know the people in this village won't turn us in?"

Slade leveled a steely gaze at him. "They won't."

I had to trust that the people in the town cared for Slade enough to be willing to hide our secret. There was no time to do anything else. "Let's go."

Our group hurried to Slade's house, where a surprised Noren opened the door. Once Slade explained what was happening, Noren ushered us inside with a worried expression. As the door shut, I heard a deep screech outside along with the heavy flap of wings, and a chill went down my spine.

Slade took the lead as he rushed us through the house, and I barely had time to glimpse dark wood furnishings before we were taken into a back bedroom. Slade and Jasin shoved the bed aside, then threw open a panel in the floor. The space inside was small and dark, but I quickly hopped down into it, my feet landing on packed dirt. My mates followed me, but Auric and Slade both had to duck down since they were too tall to comfortably fit inside. It was a tight squeeze with the five of us and the air had an old, moldy smell, but I prayed we wouldn't be stuck inside too long.

Brin and Noren helped lower the panel over us, trapping us inside, and then they shoved the bed back into place to cover it up. The cramped space instantly felt tighter, darker, and more suffocating. Auric gripped my hand tightly —he didn't like being in enclosed places like this. Slade, on the other hand, probably felt right at home.

Footsteps sounded, and then Leni's voice whispered, "Are they safe?"

"Yes," Brin said.

"The Jade Dragon just landed," Leni said. "He's searching the village for five people—one woman and four men. What will we do when he comes here?"

"We'll convince him there's no one here but us."

The Jade Dragon—here? I'd never seen Heldor in person before, even while living in the Earth Realm. He rarely left the capital of Soulspire or the Black Dragon's side, and acted as both her guardian and her right hand man. The fact that he was here likely meant that all the Dragons were looking for us—and they were desperate to find us.

Slade took my elbow and moved me over by a few inches, placing me in front of a small crack that allowed me to see some of what was going on above us. Brin and Leni were embracing, while Noren had left the room at some point.

For some time we waited. My mates shifted around me, visibly uncomfortable and anxious, but remaining quiet as the heaviness of the situation pressed upon us. I strained to hear anything from outside the house, worried I would catch a scream or a shout, but if there were any they were muffled. I silently prayed to the Gods that the Jade Dragon wouldn't find any reason to hurt the people of this town, who had shown us nothing but kind hospitality since we'd arrived. But with every second that passed, I grew more and more apprehensive.

Then I heard a low voice say, "What's behind this door?"

"A bedroom," Noren said. "Like I told you, there's no one here."

"Then why do I not believe you?"

The door to the bedroom banged open, and I couldn't help but jump. Brin and Leni let out surprised gasps from

145

the bed above us, where they must have been waiting. Heavy footsteps shook the floorboards above us as the Jade Dragon entered the room in his human form. I couldn't see much of him, but I could tell he was a large, broad man from the way he moved. For a second I got a glimpse of dark, muscular skin decorated with tattoos, along with a shaved head.

"No one here?" Heldor asked. "Then who are these two?"

"My cousin and her girlfriend," Noren said with a hint of annoyance. He moved to the bed and shooed them off it. "What have I told you before? I don't care if your families don't approve, you can't use my room for your illicit encounters. Get out of here!"

"Sorry," Leni and Brin muttered, and I caught a glimpse of their mostly naked bodies as they bent down and grabbed their clothes off the floor. They must have planned this with Noren as a distraction.

They hurried out of the room, and Noren sighed. "I apologize, my lord. They'll find anywhere to sneak off together."

Heldor let out a grunt, walked the length of the room, and then turned on his heel and stormed out without another word. I let out a relieved breath, and I sensed my mates calming too. Although none of us would be able to relax completely until the Jade Dragon had left the town and everyone was safe.

I wasn't sure how long we waited until the bed over us

was moved and the panel opened. Bright light blinded me for a moment, and then a hand reached down to help me climb out. Noren, Brin, and Leni waited for us at the top, and Leni threw her arms around her brother as he emerged.

"He's gone," Brin said.

"Did he hurt anyone?" Slade asked.

"No, he made a lot of threats and scared people pretty good, but that's it," Leni said. "I'm so glad he didn't find you."

"No one told him about us?" Reven asked, as he climbed out.

Noren puffed up his chest. "Of course not. We protect our own."

"That's very noble, especially since we've put you all at risk," Auric said.

"I never should have brought us here," Slade mumbled.

Reven brushed dust off himself. "Perhaps it's time for us to leave."

I reluctantly nodded. "Yes, with each minute we stay we put these people in greater danger."

"But we don't want you to go!" Leni said. "Having you here has been the best thing to happen to this boring town in years."

"We don't want to leave either," I said with a sigh. "But it's best for everyone if we go now, no matter how much we'd like to stay."

"Come with us," Brin said, taking Leni's hand.

Her face fell. "Gods, I want to, but my mother would never let me leave. Let alone my overbearing brother."

"I let my parents dictate my life for far too long and almost married a man I didn't love because of it." Brin glanced over at Auric apologetically, but he just shrugged. "It was hard to break free and do what I knew I needed, but it was worth it."

"She is not coming with us," Slade said. "End of discussion."

"See?" Leni said, rolling her eyes. "I'll never get out of this town."

We left Noren's house and returned to the inn to pack up our things. When we emerged, a large group waited for us with Yena at the front of it. She threw her arms around Slade, her eyes wet.

"Please be careful," she said, as she pulled back to look at him. "Come back to us once this is all done."

"I will, mother," Slade said.

Yena turned to me next and enveloped me in a hug, her arms soft and comforting. For a few seconds it reminded me of what it was like to have a mother of my own. "You be safe as well. Slade needs you."

I nodded, my throat closing up with emotion. Wrin handed us some food she had packed for us to eat on the road, while the rest of Slade's family hugged him and said their goodbyes. Many of them wished me well too, and the tightening in my chest grew worse with each goodbye. I'd had no idea I would come to care for this village so much, or that I would have such a hard time leaving it.

Leni rushed down the road with a bag thrown over her shoulder and a sword at her waist. "Don't leave without me!"

"Leni!" Yena cried out. "What do you think you are doing?"

"I'm going with them." She moved to Brin's side and stood tall. "I know you don't approve, mother, but I have to do this. I feel it in my bones. This is my destiny."

Yena pursed her lips, but then slowly nodded. "I always knew you would leave us. I only hoped I would have more time before then. Please be safe."

"Thank you, mother," Leni said, throwing her arms around Yena. "I promise I'll be careful."

"You're letting her go?" Slade asked, his face incredulous.

"I am," Yena said. "Leni is a grown woman and must make her own decisions, even if I will always worry for her. Please promise to watch over your sister, will you?"

"I'll do my best," he said with reluctance.

"More like I'll be the one watching over him," Leni said, nudging him in the side.

"We're lucky to have you," I said. "Are we ready?"

Jasin nodded, and he stepped back as his body began to change. There was no more hiding anymore, and the crowd gasped as Jasin shifted into a large red-scaled dragon before them. Some people shied back, fearing his new form, but others moved closer like they wanted a better look. Auric shifted into his own dragon form next, his golden wings bright and regal under the sun, and the crowd let out more impressed sounds.

I turned toward the crowd and raised my voice. "Thank you all for your hospitality. These past few days in your village have been some of the best of my life, and I'll cherish them always. We apologize for any danger we may have put you in, but we're impressed by your bravery and loyalty in the face of threat. We truly appreciate all you have done for us and hope to see you again one day."

I gave a short bow and then climbed onto Auric's back, while the crowd cheered and murmured behind us. Slade got on behind me, while the others clambered onto Jasin's back. Leni grinned from ear to ear as she sat in front of Brin, and I hoped we were doing the right thing by taking her with us. I didn't want any more lives on my hands, although I knew that was becoming inevitable. As the future Black Dragon, people would always follow me...and so would death.

24

KIRA

We stopped beside a small lake to camp for the evening, and I immediately missed the comforts of Clayridge, including a hot meal and a real bed. On the other hand, it eased my mind to be on the road again, knowing we were less of a threat to the villagers' safety now that we were gone.

After eating some of the food Wrin had packed for us, I retreated to the edge of the lake by myself and sat on the banks. Although I told myself I wanted time alone, I secretly hoped Enva would appear to me again, as she often did when I was troubled. The old woman could be infuriating and confusing, but she was also my grandmother and I wanted to get to know her better. But after a few minutes of staring at the smooth water she never arrived, and I gave up on that hope.

This time, it didn't surprise me when Reven emerged

and sat beside me. No matter how much he tried to keep his distance and pretend he didn't care, it hadn't escaped my notice that when I was upset and ran off to be alone with my thoughts, it was usually Reven who sought me out first to comfort me. His form of comfort might be more unconventional than the other men's, but I appreciated his presence nonetheless.

"Are you ready for tomorrow?" he asked, as he stretched out his long legs beside me.

"As ready as I can be," I replied. "I'm mostly worried about Jasin and Auric, along with the others fighting beside them at Salt Creek Tower. Our role seems easier in comparison."

"They'll be fine. They're both strong fighters and quick thinkers."

I nodded, but I wouldn't feel completely at ease until the battle was over and all the people I cared about were out of danger. Except as soon as this battle was over, we were sure to face another one soon.

"What of you?" I asked. "If we get through this, we'll be visiting the Water Temple next. Are you ready for that?"

"I'm not going to run away, if that's what you're asking." His hand rested on my knee, then slid upward in a tantalizing way that made me hold my breath.

I turned toward him, pressing softly against his hard chest. "Does that mean you've accepted your role as the next Azure Dragon?"

"I have." His strong hands wrapped around my waist,

and he pulled me onto his lap and against his chest. "I want to defeat the Dragons as much as you do. And I'll admit, the perks of the position are pretty appealing."

"What perks would those be?" I asked, suddenly breathless now that we were so close and his hands were on me. I let my fingers slide up to his neck, thrilled at being able to touch him in return.

"You." He crushed his lips against mine, kissing me hard. Weeks of pent-up desire between us was suddenly unleashed, and I tangled my fingers in his thick black hair as I kissed him back with the same passion. His tongue danced with mine, and his teeth nibbled along my lower lip. We'd kissed before, and done a lot more that one night, but this was different—because now he'd agreed to be my mate.

He pressed me down onto the grass, his body hovering over mine, and took the kiss deeper. He kissed me with his entire body and I clung to him, worried he'd back away, but he didn't this time. His hands drifted up to cup my breasts through my dress, and I let out a low moan. My legs spread to let him position himself between them, and I felt his hard bulge nudge against me. Our hips grinded together, creating a delicious friction that made me crave more.

When his hands moved down to my knees and began to slide up my bare legs, I was practically begging for him to continue. He found the slick wetness between my thighs and I looked up at him with hunger, longing to become one with him, but a part of me was surprised he wasn't stopping either.

"You don't want to wait until the Water Temple?" I asked.

"Why wait?" His mouth descended on mine again while he continued the slow grind of his hips against mine, except now he slipped a finger inside me too. "We both want this right now. Or should I stop?"

Unease mixed with my desire at his words, even though his touch made it hard for me to think. "The others all wanted to wait to bond at the temples because it would be more special that way."

"I hate to break it to you, but if you're waiting for this to be special between us, you'll be waiting forever." He lowered his head to kiss my neck as his fingers continued their delicious torment inside me. "This is just sex, that's all. But trust me, you'll enjoy it."

"Just sex?" I lightly pushed him off me and sat up. "But I thought you wanted to be my mate."

He dragged a hand through his black hair. "I agreed to sleep with you and become one of your Dragons. I'm here, I'm not leaving, and I'm committed to our cause. Isn't that enough?"

"No, it's not." I yanked my dress down to cover my legs, even though my body silently pleaded for him to continue what he'd been doing. "I want more."

"I don't have anything more to give." His eyes darkened, his mouth turning into a scowl. "I'm not capable of love, not like you want."

"I don't believe that."

"Believe it," he growled. "Long ago I watched everyone I loved die, and I'll never let myself feel that way again. Like I told you before, love makes you weak, and I won't be weak ever again."

"You're wrong. I've lost everyone too, but I haven't closed myself off because of it. Loving the others has made me stronger—and not just with magic. The other men give me confidence and courage, wisdom and empathy, and the support I need to get through all of this. The only way we'll survive the upcoming battles is with love." I reached for him again. "I'd like to love you too, Reven. Just let me in."

"It's never going to happen. You need to get that into your head already." He got up and walked away, leaving me alone and cold beside the lake with only the stars overhead for company.

A deep sadness settled over me at the thought that Reven would never love me as much as I loved him, but there was nothing I could do about it. I couldn't force his heart to let me in, and I didn't want any other man as my mate. We were stuck together, and I'd have to accept that things between us would never be exactly as I wanted. Whatever Reven offered would have to be enough...even if I would want more for the rest of my days.

25

KIRA

The next day we flew north into the mountains toward the Earth Temple. It was located on top of Frost-mount, the tallest point in the realm, although we weren't going there, not exactly. We were meeting Parin on another mountain in a cave that he said would lead us into the temple without anyone noticing. As his mother was once the High Priestess, I was inclined to believe him, even though it was hard to trust a relative stranger with something this important. But Slade seemed to trust Parin, even if he didn't like him, and I trusted Slade.

The air grew colder and colder as we approached the snow-covered mountains, and I pulled my fur-lined hood over my head. We'd bought cold weather clothing and supplies during our time in Clayridge, but I wasn't sure anything could fight off the chill here.

Auric and Jasin were careful to fly high in the clouds, and cautious when they came down to land beside the cave entrance, which was covered in frost. They shifted as soon as we were off their backs, and only then did Parin emerge from the shadows.

"I'm not sure it will ever get any less terrifying seeing two dragons flying toward me, even if I know they're my allies," Parin said, shaking his head. "But I'm glad you made it."

"Thank you for meeting us here," I said. Parin was putting his own life in danger by guiding us through these tunnels, but he'd insisted on coming with us, even though it meant leaving his people to fight without him. Faya would be leading the battle at Salt Creek Tower, and I knew he must be worried about her, just as I worried about my mates.

"Are your troops in position?" Jasin asked.

"They are," Parin said. "Everything is ready. They're simply waiting for you to join them."

"Then this is where we go our separate ways," Auric said, turning to me. He drew me in for a tight hug, then kissed me softly on the lips. "Be careful, Kira."

"You too." My heart clenched, knowing I was sending two of my mates into danger, and that I wouldn't be there to protect them. They probably felt the same about leaving me.

Jasin grabbed me in his warm embrace next, kissing me hard. "I'll look after Auric. Don't worry."

"Thank you. I know he'll look out for you too." I reached

out and grabbed both their hands, connecting us again and feeling the bond surge between the three of us. "I love you both."

My two mates replied that they loved me too, and after more kisses they finally stepped back. I hugged Brin next, making her promise to stay safe, and overheard Slade talking to his sister in a low voice.

"You don't have to fight," he said. "It's not too late to back out."

"I want to fight," Leni said, standing taller.

He hugged her tight and seemed reluctant to let her go. Then he turned back to Jasin and Auric. "Take care of my sister for me."

"We will, I promise," Jasin said.

"As if she were our own blood," Auric promised.

As the goodbyes finished, I retreated to stand between Slade and Reven. Slade's hand rested on my lower back as worry made me bite my lower lip, and together we watched as Jasin and Auric returned to their glorious dragon forms. With a few flaps of their wings they were in the air again, and then they were gone.

"They'll be fine," Reven said. We'd avoided each other since last night, and I still felt a pang of sadness when I remembered what had happened, but I had to get past that now.

"I hope so." With a sigh, I turned toward the cave. According to Parin we had a long hike ahead of us through the icy tunnels, and standing here worrying about the others wouldn't accomplish anything.

"Follow me," Parin said, as he led us into the darkness.

26

AURIC

After hours of flying we reached the rendezvous point, a cave near Salt Creek Tower where the Resistance had gathered. Brin and Leni hopped off and removed the supplies from our backs, and then we shifted into our human forms again. I popped my shoulders, which were always a bit stiff after using my wings, while the others checked their weapons. Even though I was likely to remain a dragon for much of the battle, I strapped on my own long, curved daggers, a gift from my father that had been in our family for centuries, passed down from the brother of the first Golden Dragon.

A somber mood had settled over all of us, both from leaving Kira and the others behind, along with the upcoming battle we were about to face. Brin and Leni laced their hands together and spoke in quiet voices, though I had no doubt they'd be ready to fight. Brin was an excellent warrior, and I'd heard she'd been helping Leni train too. If Leni was half as dangerous as her brother, she'd be a formidable force.

"The Earth Realm sure likes its caves," Jasin muttered, as he strode toward the entrance. Brin and Leni followed a few steps behind him.

I kept pace with him. "Perhaps that's why the Resistance has the largest presence here. Easier to hide from the Dragons."

Jasin shrugged, and we stepped inside the damp, dark cave. As my eyes adjusted to the dim light, I took in the sight of dozens of warriors gathered, with more stretching back into tunnels and out of view. Parin had promised us a hundred men and women, armed with bows, axes, swords, and more.

Faya pushed her way to the front of the crowd. Last time I'd seen her she'd worn slim, simple dresses, but now she was geared for combat in silver armor with a large sword strapped to her back. After visiting the quiet town she'd grown up in, I could see why she had felt stifled there.

"We're ready to begin moving out," she said. "At your command, we'll begin the attack."

We quickly went over the plan again, clarifying a few things, while Jasin and I chugged water and shoved food into our mouths for energy. Once we were ready, we moved outside of the cave, while the fighters began to head toward the fort.

I turned toward Jasin and clasped his hand in my own. "Good luck today, my friend."

"You too." He drew me in for a quick embrace, and we gave each other a tight squeeze. "I've got your back out there."

"And I've got yours."

As we pulled apart, I keenly felt the connection between us, even without Kira here. And from the way he met my eyes, I knew he felt it too.

I turned to Brin next, then wrapped her in a close hug. My oldest friend, my former fiancé, and now my close companion on this strange journey. I had no idea if this thing with her and Leni would work out, but I was happy she'd found someone who made her smile. "Take care of yourself, okay?"

"I always do," she said with a wry grin. "Don't get yourself killed either."

I chuckled softly. "I'll do my best."

I gave Leni a nod, and then the two women joined the ranks of the other warriors. I'd be watching for them from above, trying to keep them safe, and I knew Jasin would be doing the same.

I became a dragon once more, feeling my body shift and grow, along with the rush of power that came from the transformation. My skin became scales, my hands became talons, and my teeth became fangs. Great, golden wings spread from my body, and with a mighty roar I launched into the air, with Jasin at my side.

Together we flew toward Salt Creek Tower to begin the assault, while the Resistance's fighters surged forward. According to Faya, she'd already sent a few men and women to sneak into the fort itself, and they would open the gate for us. If they failed, Jasin and I would have to get it down somehow.

The fort came into view, consisting of a few stone buildings with a large wall around it surrounded by a narrow moat. Onyx Army soldiers in their black armor lined the top of the wall, and they let out a shout when they saw us coming. Our fighters spread out in front of the wall, while the soldiers inside the fort prepared for battle.

Jasin gave me a nod, smoke already coming from his nostrils, and then flew forward. I hung back and circled low over the Resistance fighters. We'd decided Jasin would lead the offensive, focusing on taking out as many of the soldiers in the fort as possible, while I'd help defend our own people. Partly because his magic was better suited for an attack, and partly because I'd never been in a battle like this before, while Jasin had seen plenty of them. I was no stranger to combat, but warfare was an entirely new experience for me.

Jasin glided over the fort and let out a loud, terrifying roar that hit me all the way in my bones. I opened my mouth and released one of my own in response, signaling the attack was to begin—and hopefully sending fear into our enemies.

The heavy metal gate at the front of the fort opened, and our fighters surged forward into the keep with a loud cry. At the same time, Jasin unleashed a stream of red hot fire, taking out a line of soldiers on the wall. The ones he missed launched arrows at our people, but with a blast of air I sent them flying back to the archers.

Below us, people met in battle with a clash of swords and the spilling of blood. I caught sight of Brin and Leni fighting back to back, cutting down their opponents with ease. When a man leveled a spear at them, I dove down and caught it in my talons, then drove it through his chest. My tail whipped around, knocking two other soldiers down, and I began slashing with talons and teeth, while blasting out air strong enough to knock others back.

I don't know how long this continued, or how many we killed or lost in combat. My scales and claws grew slick with blood, but I kept fighting while Jasin continued to set the fort on fire all around us. And then I heard a terrible screech overhead that stopped me in my tracks.

I glanced up to see two dragons swooping down to oppose us, one with blood-red scales and the other's the deepest green. Just as I'd expected—Sark, the Crimson Dragon, and Heldor, the Jade Dragon. The ones who'd destroyed Kira's town with lava, earthquakes, and fire. And now we had to hold them off as long as possible so Kira and Slade could finish the bonding.

As I flew up to meet the other dragons in combat, I opened myself to my bond with Kira and sent her a single, frantic feeling: *Go!*

27

KIRA

I pulled my fur cloak tighter around myself, wishing I'd brought even warmer clothes. Only the flame rising from my palm emitted any warmth—or light—inside the dark, frosty cave.

We'd been going uphill in the tunnel for what seemed like hours, although it was impossible to tell. The walls were unnaturally smooth, like in the Resistance base, but there were few other signs that anyone had been this way before and no way to tell if we were going in the right direction. Parin led us forward and claimed to know where he was going, and Slade pressed his hand to the rock and then nodded, but it was still eerie facing step after step of nothing but cold, dark stone.

"We're almost there," Parin said, an eternity later. "We should stop here until we get the signal."

I sank against the wall, my body eager to take a break.

There was nothing to do now but wait and pray our plan worked. I closed my eyes and reached for Jasin and Auric to reassure myself they were all right, but I found a wild mix of emotions that threatened to overwhelm me. They were still alive, and I had to accept that that was enough for now.

"How much farther to the temple?" Reven asked.

"Not far now." Parin leaned against the side of the tunnel opposite me, his face grim. "I forgot to mention...we received a report that the Water Temple has been destroyed by the Dragons too. There's nothing left. I'm sorry."

I drew in a deep breath and nodded. The news made my heart sink, but I couldn't focus on that now. I'd known getting to the Water Temple would be difficult and it had just become even more impossible, but we had to face one challenge at a time. Besides, I couldn't even think about bonding with Reven at the moment. I was still too bruised after last night. "Thanks for letting me know."

We sipped water and ate some of the food we'd brought with us while we waited. Slade paced back and forth, while Reven became so still I almost wondered if he was asleep. I tried not to fret over how the others were faring in their battle, but it was difficult.

Suddenly Auric's presence filled my mind and I felt him urging me to move, to go, to hurry. I scrambled to my feet. "I got the signal!"

We jumped back into action, our bodies recovered after the break, and continued forward with Parin at the lead. The plan had worked, but we had to hurry since we didn't know how long the Resistance could keep the Dragons away. Eventually they would realize this was a distraction and come back to stop us. We needed to be finished by then.

Parin stopped in front of a spot in the wall that looked like it had caved in at some point. Water flowed through the cracks in the rocks in a steady trickle, pooling around our feet. "The temple is through here, but I've never seen this water before."

"I can move the rocks," Slade said, stepping forward.

"Wait." Reven crouched down, dipped his finger into the water, and stared at the cracks where it was coming from. When he straightened up, he said, "The room on the other side has been flooded. When you open it up, I'll divert the water away."

"The Azure Dragon must have done this to keep us out," Parin mumbled.

"Most likely," Slade said.

Reven instructed us to stand to the side with our backs against the stone, and then nodded at Slade. The rocks began to slide away from the wall, slowly at first, allowing larger bursts of water to break through. Soon they began to tumble down much faster, and a huge wall of water rushed out. Reven raised his hands and stopped the water from hitting us, then sent it flowing through the tunnel where we'd already been. It filled the entire passage, a great torrent racing down the mountain like it was desperate to escape. Slade formed the rocks into a small dam, helping Reven block the water from hitting us as it roared by.

Eventually the flood slowed to a mere trickle, and it was safe enough through the gap Slade had made. It opened to a large cavern with shining wet stone and rocks that dripped cold water in a steady pattern. I raised the flames I'd summoned and gaped as the light caught on hundreds of sparkling crystals built into the walls, which shimmered all around us in every color of the rainbow. A large jade green dragon statue had toppled over in the middle of the room, it's head cracked and one of the wings shattered.

"This is the Earth Temple," Parin said, bowing his head. "Or it was."

"It's beautiful," I whispered, as I stepped forward and touched one of the glittering jewels. Even with evidence of the Dragons' destruction here and the missing priests, I could feel the magic of the temple all around me.

"This is where they killed my mother, along with her priests." Parin ran his hand along the wing of the dragon statue as we took it all in.

"Including your father?" I asked softly.

"No, he died a few years ago. Perhaps that is a blessing."

"We'll honor their sacrifice by completing our duty to the Earth God," Slade said.

Parin nodded and led us forward. Our boots squished and splashed in the leftover puddles as we walked around the rubble and debris. He took us through another tunnel, leading to a splintered, soaked door. "The bonding chamber is through here. I'm sorry it's not in better condition."

I peered through the crack in the door at the room inside. "It's not the most romantic place, but it'll do."

"We'll wait outside and stand guard," Reven said.

While they retreated back to the main part of the temple, Slade opened the broken door with a loud creak. My heart probably should have sank at the sight of the remains of the bed, which had been completely torn apart and turned to splinters, or the knowledge that we had to rush through this. But I was finally going to bond with Slade, and I couldn't help the small smile on my lips as I turned toward him. "Are you ready?"

He reached out and took my hand. "I am."

We stepped inside together and surveyed the destruction. It was hard to tell what furniture had once been in the room since all that remained was wreckage. The only thing that still stood was a gray marble table against one wall. Slade led me to it, while his magic slammed the door shut behind us.

Anticipation made my desire and excitement even stronger, and when he took me in his arms and kissed me, my heart leaped. He nudged me back until my behind hit the edge of the table, and then he eased me up onto the edge of the cool stone. The position lifted me up higher, allowing me to kiss him easier while my arms circled his neck. My knees spread wide and he moved between them, his hard, muscular length pressed against me.

"I wish we didn't have to rush," he said, as his hands slid down to my breasts, slowly rubbing my nipples through the fabric of my dress. "I wanted to go slow and take all night learning your body and what makes you sigh. This will be the first time I've made love to a woman in many years and I'd hoped to savor it, especially since it's you."

His words sent a rush of warmth to my core as I imagined all the things we would do together. "Next time we'll take as long as you want, I promise."

"Yes," he said, with hunger in his eyes. "Next time."

His mouth descended on mine again and I pressed against him, my body throbbing with desire. Soft lips trailed over my earlobe and down my neck to my collarbone, nuzzling and tasting, and I closed my eyes with a sigh. But then I felt Auric and Jasin reaching for each other's magic through the bond, their emotions a mix of frenzy, fear, and determination, and I knew we had to hurry. Slade's seductive touch made me want to take my time too, but we couldn't forget that others were fighting and dying for us to have this moment.

I reached for Slade's shirt and lifted it over his head, revealing his dark, muscular chest. I drank in the sight of the sculpted lines of his body, all the smooth planes and hard ridges just begging for my touch. When I reached out and lightly ran my hand along those muscles he let out a ragged breath, and then claimed my mouth again. While we kissed, his fingers caressed down my hips and gripped the fabric of my dress, then inched it up my legs. My breath hitched with excitement, but then he pulled back and met my eyes.

"There's something I need to say first." His hands slid

along my bare thighs as he spoke, his deep, sensual voice wrapping around me like a blanket. "I gave away my heart once and had it broken. I never thought I would ever love again, and didn't want to even try. And then I met you..." He drew in a breath, his fingers tightening on my skin. "I didn't want to love you either. I tried to resist you for so long. But there was no use. I fell for you anyway." His head bent, his brow pressing against mine. "I love you, Kira."

I brushed my fingers against his jaw, while my heart felt like it would burst out of my chest. "I love you too, Slade."

"You somehow mended my heart and showed me it was possible to love again. Even if the Gods didn't demand I spend my life with you, I would do it anyway." He dropped to his knees in front of me. "I'm yours."

He was the biggest and strongest of my mates. He could crush me both with his magic or without it. And now he was kneeling in front of me. There was nothing sexier than seeing such a powerful man on his knees before me, and the space between my legs softly ached with need.

He coaxed my thighs to spread wider for him, his green eyes moving to gaze at the place that throbbed for his touch, and I knew what he planned to do.

Even as my body said *oh please yes*, I rested a hand on his shoulder to stop him. "We don't have time."

"I don't care. I'm going to taste you, even if only for a moment. I've been thinking of little else for days."

Stubborn man. I knew I should tell him no, that we needed to hurry, but I wanted his mouth on me, that lush, full mouth I'd been tempted by since we'd met. When his head dipped down and I felt the roughness of his beard against my inner thighs, all my protests were silenced. I forgot about everything except his mouth as it pressed against me and his tongue as it stroked me. I leaned back, my hands planted on the table, as he hooked my legs over his shoulders and began to feast upon me.

My eyes fluttered closed, my breathing grew rough, and every nerve in my body seemed to burst into song. With each firm stroke of his tongue and soft touch of his lips I lost myself even more. Slade loved me, he truly loved me, and he showed me over and over how devoted he was to me. *Me*, not his duty to the Earth God or as the next Jade Dragon, just me. And I could finally admit how much I loved him too.

I cried out, my legs trembling, as the orgasm shook through me like an earthquake. Slade held my hips in place as he wrung every last drop of pleasure out of me. Only then did he release me and straighten up again—and when our eyes met I knew it was time for him to truly claim me.

2 8

JASIN

All around us the battle raged, but Auric and I focused on the two Dragons in front of us. We'd been dodging blows and throwing magic for the last few minutes, keeping them distracted as best we could while our people fought below us. As long as we kept the Dragons busy, Kira and Slade would be able to bond. I just hoped they were quick about it.

Sark spat a ball of fire at Auric, and I pressed my wings close and dove to block it. The flames struck my scaled chest and I absorbed the magic into my own body, then let out a loud roar in response. I briefly felt Auric's gratitude through the bond, before Heldor collided with me. He was the largest dragon I'd ever seen, and he slammed us both to the ground with his massive strength. We slid through the dirt, knocking soldiers back with our wings and tails, before smashing into the stone wall surrounding the fort. I tore at him with my talons and fangs, then managed to roll out from under his grasp. I backed up and let out a stream of fire from my mouth, but he yanked rocks from the wall to block my magic.

The ground underneath me shook and tore open, and I leaped into the sky again, where Sark and Auric were battling. I expected the Jade Dragon to follow me, but instead he stomped his feet and released a deep roar that made the soldiers around him balk. Lava began to spew from the newly formed crack in the ground, spraying the men and women nearby—both our fighters and the enemy's. Heldor didn't seem to care who he hit, and lava began to flow in a massive wave, threatening to cut down every person in its path, regardless of who they fought for.

"You'll kill your own soldiers!" I called out.

Heldor ignored me and continued on, making the crack wider to take up the length of the entire courtyard. People screamed and ran, the battle momentarily forgotten as they tried to escape the red hot magma, but some of them were too slow in their armor and were pulled down and consumed. How could he do this to his own people, the ones he'd come out here to defend? Did he care nothing at all for their lives?

I fought back the lava and the flames as best I could, trying to give people time to escape, but it wasn't enough. We had to stop the Dragons.

I reached for Auric through the bond, while glancing up at his shining form. He darted above me, performing whip-fast acrobatics in the air to avoid Sark's flames. Through our many hours of training we'd gotten a lot better at this, and had learned that proximity was most important, but visual contact helped too. I felt Auric acknowledge me and mentally clasp my hands. His magic mingled with mine, and I focused on Heldor and released it.

A giant lightning bolt shot from the clouds and struck the Jade Dragon on his large scaled head, and he staggered back like he was dazed. Auric threw some lightning at Sark above me too, although the other dragon was able to dodge the blast. Without Isen nearby, Sark would be unable to create lightning of his own, and we kept up the assault, paying him back for the attack at the Air Temple.

I heard Faya's voice call out for a retreat, and caught sight of Brin staggering toward the gate with one arm around Leni. Lava blocked their path, and I used my magic to remove the heat from it, turning it to stone. They rushed over it and out of the fort, hopefully on their way to safety.

Heldor recovered from the lightning bolt and threw more rocks at me, which I dodged. Mostly. One huge boulder struck my left wing, clipping it and shooting pain through my shoulder. I swore under my breath and leaped into the air, but each beat of my wings was agony.

I crashed back down to the ground and Heldor let out a deep, throaty laugh as he approached. Auric dropped down in front of him, blocking my body with his own, and launched another bolt of lightning at Heldor. It struck him in the chest, knocking him back, and the huge green dragon slumped to the ground.

"Jasin, are you injured?" Auric asked.

I stood up and shook myself off, but pain shot through me. "I'll be all right. I'm not sure I can fly though. I'll need Kira to heal me later."

A harsh shriek filled the air, and Auric and I both looked up as Isen, the Golden Dragon, swooped down toward us. Where had he come from? And could we really defend against three dragons, especially now that I was injured? I bared my teeth and readied my wings. We didn't have a choice but to fight.

I sent fire up at Isen, but he dodged easily, his nimble form darting through the sky. A tornado formed over us, whipping up all the debris on the ground, and Auric flew up to stop it. I bit back the pain and dodged the swirling, rushing winds before they surrounded me, but my injured wing slowed me down and prevented me from taking off. I managed to knock a soldier in black armor out of the way with my tail before he was caught up in the tornado, just before it dissipated.

The air around us cleared—and that's when I realized Sark and Heldor were both gone.

29

KIRA

Slade quickly removed my clothes and tossed them aside, then gazed at me with hungry eyes. I sat on the edge of the table, completely bared to him, while the echoes of pleasure made my body loose and limp. Yet I still craved more.

"I've never wanted any woman the way I want you," he said, as he dropped his trousers to the floor. I got a glimpse of his huge, hard cock before he moved between my thighs and nudged it against my core. Later I would explore every inch of him in great detail with my hands and my mouth, but for now I needed him inside me. I wrapped my arms around his neck and pulled him closer, finding his mouth again while his long length entered me.

He was big, almost too big, but I didn't want him to stop. My hips strained toward him, begging for more, but once he was fully inside he paused. He was as hard as the marble under me, pulsing with strength and need, and I thought I would die if he didn't move soon.

I caressed the smooth slope of his back down to the rounded curve of his behind, then gripped him tight, pulling him deeper inside. "Slade, please."

At my words, he let out a ragged breath and unleashed the desire that he'd kept locked inside so long. He pushed me down so I lay flat against the cool stone table, his strong hands circling my waist, and then he began to pump into me with sure, steady strokes. I gasped and lifted my hips in time to his movements, while he gazed down at me with a look of pure, ravenous lust.

My legs wrapped around Slade's hips as he stood over me, my breasts rocking with each deep glide of his cock. He took me thoroughly, possessing me completely, making me his woman with every thrust.

When he arched over me to take one of my nipples in his mouth, I couldn't help but cry out. He thrust faster, deeper, his movements becoming frantic, and I tangled my fingers in his thick hair and gave myself up to him. Release found me first and I gasped as the sensations crashed over me, my body tightening around him. He let out a low groan as he pounded into me harder, and the room around us began to tremble. I clung to Slade's shoulders, but his skin had turned to stone, and I realized with a start that mine had too. But he didn't stop, and pleasure quaked through us both without end.

When he finally calmed, our skin returned to normal

and the room stilled. Slade relaxed on top of me, and I enjoyed the feel of his strong body in my arms, pressing down on me. His lips melted against mine and love shimmered between us like one of the crystals on the walls.

"I wish I could hold you like this for hours and fall asleep with you in my arms," Slade said, as he reluctantly released me. "But we should probably leave the temple in case the Dragons return soon."

I sighed as reality came crashing back down, and all my worries about my other mates returned. "You're right, although the Earth God should come speak with us first. The other ones did, at least."

"Even more reason for us to dress then," he said, grabbing his trousers off the floor.

As soon as we'd donned our clothes, the temple began to rumble again, like it had when the bonding had completed. Only now it grew more intense, to the point where I had to hold onto the table to steady myself.

Suddenly the floor split open in front of us, and Slade rested a hand on my shoulder as if to protect me. A huge talon appeared at the edge of the crack, and then a giant dragon clawed his way out of the crevice. His body was made entirely of crystal, like the ones embedded in the walls, and when he moved his scales shifted colors like a rainbow shining across his skin. I'd never seen anything more beautiful before.

The Earth God was so large that Slade and I had to press against the wall behind us to have any space at all. His wings arched behind his back and we dropped to our knees before him as his sheer physical power and strength filled the room. I'd met two Gods before, but I'd never lost that sense of awe and wonder when confronting one.

He took us in with eyes that seemed to be made of the blackest opals, while his huge tail whipped about, tossing stones and splintered wood aside. "My avatar and my descendant. Your bonding pleases me."

Slade bowed his head. "We are your humble servants, my lord."

The crystal dragon's eyes lifted and took in the room, then seemed to see beyond it into the main temple. He let out a growl that made the mountain quake, and his tail smashed harder against the ground. "Those traitorous Dragons have destroyed my temple and murdered my priests. They must be overthrown." Those deep, black eyes focused on us again. "You must bring balance to the world."

"We're trying," I said. "But we don't know how to defeat the others. We're not strong enough yet."

"You will grow stronger the closer you become to your mates," the Earth God said. "But you already knew this."

I nodded, relieved to hear that my instinct in bringing both Auric and Jasin into my bed together was the right one. The two of them wouldn't be a problem, but the other two would be more of a challenge. I felt closer to Slade than ever before, but I wasn't sure if he would ever agree to truly share me with the others. And Reven had made it clear he only wanted a physical relationship, nothing more.

The Earth God lowered himself to the ground, stretching his silvery talons out before him like a lazy, fat cat. "The Black Dragon and her mates are no longer as close as they once were. They are fractured and splintered. Doubt and distance threaten to divide them. If you and your Dragons become a strong, cohesive group, you will become more powerful than they are."

Easier said than done, but I would do my best to bring them all together. Of course, that only solved one of our problems. "But the Black Dragon is immortal and has the power of the Spirit Goddess, plus the magic of all of her mates. How can we stop her?"

"You must defeat each of her mates first. Once you do, she will lose their powers and strengths. Only then will she be weak enough to overcome."

That meant we'd have to take them down one by one before facing her, in order to stand a chance. My stomach twisted at the idea, and it took me a second to realize it was because it meant killing both of my parents in the process. I despised them and everything they did, but they were still my blood. "My father...do you know who he is?"

"No, but I can tell you he is not my Dragon. It must be one of the others."

My heart sank. I'd been hoping the Earth God could tell me who he was, or at least confirm he wasn't the Crimson Dragon. Sark had killed the people who had raised me, and if he was my true father, I wasn't sure how I would ever be able to live with that.

"You must continue your voyage now," the Earth God said, as he rose to his feet and shook out his wings. "Remember that the fate of the world journeys with you, as do the Gods' blessings."

"Thank you for your wisdom," Slade said. "And for choosing me to be your Dragon."

The Earth God gave us a nod, and then his wings tucked tight and he dove straight into the crevice. It closed up behind him, leaving no trace he was ever there. Slade and I let out a collective held breath—and then we heard a shout from the other room.

Slade pressed his hand against the nearest wall and closed his eyes, and I knew he must be spreading his senses throughout the cave as he'd done before.

His eyes snapped open. "The Jade Dragon is here."

30

REVEN

I was leaning against the fallen statue of the Earth God and trying to ignore the way the mountain kept shaking, when something made me reach for my twin swords. A flicker of movement. A change in the air. A sense that danger was coming.

I'd stayed alive this long by trusting my instincts, and I wasn't about to stop now. I gestured at Parin, who crouched down in the debris while I moved into the shadow of the dragon statue.

Three men walked inside, and I sensed their power immediately. Sark, with hair so pale it was almost white, Heldor, as large and broad as Slade except covered in tattoos, and a third man I'd seen only once before in his human form—Doran, the Azure Dragon. He had blond hair hanging past his shoulders and a matching beard, with skin that spoke of many hours under the sun. All three of them were in their human forms, probably because the cave entrance was too small for them to get through as dragons. Each was dressed in black leather fit for fighting or traveling, but none carried weapons.

"We're too late," Doran said, his voice icy cold. "They've already left."

Heldor shook his head. "No, I sensed the earth moving. They must still be here."

"If they are, they won't be leaving," Sark growled.

My hands tightened on the hilt of my swords at his voice, but I couldn't let my rage or my need for vengeance consume me. I wasn't sure if Kira and Slade were finished or not, but I had to hold these three off as long as I could—and Parin would likely be no help. It was just me, a former assassin with a bit of magic, against three immortal Dragons. I didn't like these odds.

"Fine, let's look around," Doran said, sounding bored.

I waited until the three of them split apart, then I crept into position. As Doran passed by, I lunged out with my sword—but he quickly dodged it. He spun around, a blade made of ice forming in his hands, and blocked my next blow with it.

"Found one," he called out to the others.

We struck and parried, beginning a complicated dance of swords, while the others moved closer. Sark let loose a blast of fire at me, but I ducked under it, while Heldor grabbed rocks leftover from the temple's destruction and hurled them at me. I threw up a wall of ice to block them, then continued my assault on the man I would soon replace. Doran moved with the grace of a seasoned fighter and was as fast as I was, providing me a challenge. If it were just the two of us I thought I could probably best him, but all three of them? Even I wasn't that good.

I sensed Sark moving behind me, and realized I was surrounded. But then Parin let out a shout as he lunged from the corner and struck Sark with his sword from behind. Sark let out a roar and grabbed Parin by the neck, instantly lighting him on fire. The man's horrifying screams echoed throughout the cave, and I summoned water to douse him, but it only dulled Sark's flames for a moment before they sprang up again. With Doran and Heldor both attacking me, and Sark's hand around Parin's throat, the man didn't stand a chance.

But then Sark was knocked back by a strong blast of air, which also snuffed out the fire covering Parin's body. Kira and Slade stood at the side of the cave, and they didn't waste any time joining the fight. Slade grabbed some of the boulders around the room and sent them to knock Doran down, freeing me to throw knives of ice at Heldor. Three against three—I liked those odds a lot better.

Magic flew and swords flashed as the fight broke out across the ruined temple. Kira faced Sark down with a look of pure hatred in her eyes, throwing both air and rocks at him. At least the bonding was completed in time. Now all we had to do was escape.

A section of the cave suddenly broke apart and crashed

down on top of me. Slade turned and caught it in time, stopping Heldor's magic with his own. Lava erupted in front of Sark at the same moment, making Kira step back with a gasp. Doran moved behind her, his movements swift and decisive, and caught her arm. He pressed something across her mouth and nose, a cloth of some sort. From my days as an assassin I knew it had to be some sort of poison or intoxicant. Probably nightwillow oil, which could knock a grown man out in seconds—I'd used it before to incapacitate people I had no interest in killing.

Kira tried to fight, but she was caught off guard and trapped between Sark and Doran. I called out and lunged toward her, but lava sprang up all around me and Slade, keeping us away. She struggled for a few seconds while Slade and I desperately tried to put out the molten lava flowing around us, and then her body went limp. She collapsed against Doran, and there was nothing we could do to stop it.

The Azure Dragon swooped Kira into his arms and began walking out of the cave with her. Sark and Heldor turned toward us to make sure we couldn't follow, and the lava suddenly leaped up—directly at Slade.

I knocked him out of the way, throwing up a wall of ice at the same time. Some of the lava still got through and splashed against my side, making me hiss from the burning pain. My magic put it out, but the damage was already done.

Sark turned and followed after Doran, leaving only Heldor behind. I clutched my burning side and turned to face the remaining Dragon, while calling out to Slade, who was getting to his feet.

"Go!" I said. "You're the only one who can save Kira now!"

Slade hesitated, glancing between me and Heldor, before nodding. His magic would be useless against Heldor anyway, and he could fly and I couldn't. We both knew this was what had to be done.

Slade created a bridge of rocks over the lava and dashed across them, while Heldor made the cave around me quake. Rocks and crystals fell as Slade ran, and I threw bolts of ice at Heldor to distract him. As Slade reached the cave's exit, he glanced back one more time at me. I could see from his eyes that the decision haunted him, but Kira was more important than any of us. He knew this as well as I did, and he finally turned and ran down the tunnel, leaving me to my fate.

It was just me and Heldor now, and if these were my last moments alive, I wasn't going out without a fight. I reached deep inside myself, finding that connection to the Water God I'd once tried so hard to escape from, and let it free. Cold water rained down from the roof of the cave, turning the lava to sizzling black stone. As Heldor tried to go after Slade, I closed up the cave entrance with a wall of thick, glimmering ice.

"Not so fast," I said.

The Jade Dragon turned back to me, his face hard. I limped forward, shooting shards of frost his way, but he knocked them all aside. He gestured and the ceiling above me ripped apart and came tumbling down. I threw up some ice to stop it, but knew it wouldn't be enough, not when the entire cave began to break apart over me.

The air grew thick with dirt and stone as it rained down on me, and even my strongest magic couldn't stop an entire mountain from collapsing on my head. No matter how I tried to hold up the stones above me, they soon surrounded me, striking me and rendering me immobile.

As the world around me went dark, my last thought was that I should have told Kira how I truly felt about her—and now I'd never have that chance.

31

SLADE

I rushed through the cave after Kira, my heart pounding and my chest tight. I couldn't lose her, not when I'd only just bonded with her. She was everything to me, even if it had taken me far too long to realize it, and I'd be damned if I was going to let the Dragons steal her away.

When I reached the cave's entrance, scalding hot air burned my skin. Steam, I realized, as I stumbled back. Created by Sark and Doran together, no doubt as a way to slow me down. Through the foggy haze I saw the two Dragons flying high, up into the clouds, already a good distance away—taking Kira with them.

I let out a guttural roar as my body began to shift and change, growing larger and forming scales, forming wings and a tail. Power and strength filled me like nothing before, and I felt as though I could take on anything and survive. Like two other Dragons.

I forced my way back out into the burning steam, my scales offering some protection from the scalding heat, and when I reached the edge I stretched out my wings. I pictured Jasin and Auric flying and tried to copy what they'd done, but couldn't lift off the ground. I drew in another boiling breath of hot, humid air, and tried again. Why wasn't this working? Auric had been able to fly immediately, and Jasin had picked it up almost as fast. I didn't understand what I was doing wrong. And with every second, Kira got farther away.

I tried everything I could think of to fly, moving my wings in all sorts of different ways, but the best I got was a foot or two up before my huge body dragged me back down. It was like my wings weren't strong enough to carry me. Frustration made me growl and roar, my tail slamming into the earth and sending rocks flying, but it was useless. I'd never catch her at this rate.

The mountain began to cave in behind me, the ground under me quaking, and then a hole burst open in the side of it. The Jade Dragon flew out of it, soaring over me, and then headed up into the clouds. I tried once more to follow him, with no success. And behind me, the mountain continued to collapse—with Reven still inside it.

I'd left him behind, knowing it might mean his doom, and I hadn't even been able to go after Kira. Indecision and frustration tore at me. I hated giving up on Kira, but I had no way of following after her. My wings were useless, and I knew this failure would haunt me forever, but there was still something I could do to save Kira's last mate.

I let out one final, angry roar and turned back toward the mountain to save Reven.

Auric and Jasin arrived while I was using my last reserves of magic to uncover the rubble that had crushed Reven. By now I didn't hold onto any hope that he was still alive, but I had to do something. Especially since Kira was gone, and my dragon form had failed me when I'd tried to go after her. Parin was dead too, his skin blackened and charred from Sark's flames. I'd held no love for the man, especially after he'd taken the first woman I'd loved, but I'd respected him and his cause. None of that mattered now though. I'd failed him too.

"What happened to you?" Jasin asked, noticing my burnt skin, a gift from the steam Sark and Doran had left behind. Jasin didn't look much better though—he clutched his arm and walked stiffly, as if he was injured. "And where's Kira?"

Auric was only a step behind Jasin. "Is she all right? Did you complete the bonding?"

I sat back on my heels and wiped dirty sweat off my brow. "She's gone. The Dragons took her."

Jasin's eyes practically bulged out of his head. "What do you mean, gone?"

I bowed my head, the shame and guilt overpowering me. "I couldn't stop them."

The others were silent as my words sank in. Jasin began to pace, tearing at his auburn hair like he was possessed, while Auric stared at the wall for so long it started to worry me.

"If they kidnapped her then they want her alive," Auric finally said. "We still have time to rescue her."

Jasin stopped pacing. "Right. We'll be able to find her through the bond. Although I don't feel anything right now."

I sat back on my heels. "They did something to Kira. Knocked her out with something. Maybe that's why."

"Maybe," Auric said, and then glanced around. "Where's Reven?"

I gestured to the rubble in front of me. "I've been trying to dig him out for the last few minutes."

Auric stared at the huge pile of rocks in horror. "He's under there?"

I nodded. Guilt tore me apart once again. "He saved my life, and then he told me to go, knowing it would likely mean his death. Why would he do that?"

"Because we're brothers," Jasin said, resting a hand on my shoulder. "Come on, we'll help you dig him out. And then we'll find Kira."

Auric offered me some water, which I gladly chugged, and then I returned to the task at hand. I used my magic to pull the rubble away, while Auric used air to help lift the smaller rocks. Jasin explained that he'd been injured during his battle with the Dragons and couldn't do much in the way of lifting, but he created a fire in the middle of the room, preventing us from freezing as the night grew colder.

I rolled away a large boulder, and spotted a strand of black hair. "He's here!"

The three of us worked together to carefully remove the rest of the rocks covering Reven's body, worried if we moved them too fast it would cause another collapse in the tunnel and possibly hurt him more. It took us a long time, and we worked solemnly, knowing we would likely find only a corpse.

When we dragged Reven's body out, it was rock hard and bitterly cold. His clothes were torn and his side was charred, his skin burnt off where he'd been hit by the lava. He'd given his life to protect me and Kira. Gods, how was I going to break it to her that one of her mates was dead and it was all my fault?

But as I sat back, I noticed something odd. Reven's body was encased in a layer of ice, which covered him like armor from head to toe, protecting him from the world around him. The others crouched beside us, staring at him.

Auric pressed his head to Reven's frosty chest and listened. "He's still alive. Barely."

Jasin rubbed his hands together and reached for Reven. "Perfect. I'll warm him up, while you see if you can get more air into his lungs."

"No!" Auric said, shoving Jasin's hands away. "The ice

is the only thing keeping him alive. If we warm him up, he'll die."

"Are you sure?" I asked, frowning at the ice-covered body. Keeping him in such a state seemed unnatural, but what did I know?

Auric nodded. "He's too badly injured. I'm shocked he's still alive as it is, but he must have summoned the ice to protect himself as the cave collapsed. But now the only one who can heal him is Kira."

I clenched my fists. "We have to rescue her."

"Yes, you do," a male voice said from the shadows. "But you can't do it alone."

We turned toward the sound, reaching for our weapons and our magic, and saw a man standing in front of us, though he stayed out of the light. Something about the way he stood was familiar, but I couldn't see his face, only that he had longer hair.

"Stay back!" Jasin yelled, drawing his sword.

"Who are you?" Auric asked.

The man's deep voice echoed through the cave. "I'm the Azure Dragon, and I'm here to help you rescue Kira."

Anger leaped into my throat and the ground quaked under my feet in response. "You were the one who took her," I growled. "Why would you help us?"

The man stepped forward and the light from the fire illuminated his face, revealing hazel eyes. Kira's eyes. "Because I'm her father."

32

KIRA

I forced my eyes open, though my eyelids felt as if they were made of stone. My entire body ached, and when I moved I realized it was because I was crumpled on the ground on my side. My vision was blurred, but as I sat up and blinked, the world slowly came into focus again.

The first thing I noticed were the bones. They surrounded me, forming a cage around my body just large enough for me to stand inside, and I was pretty sure they were human. The gleaming white bones crisscrossed over and under me, although the sides of my new, morbid prison had large enough gaps for me to see through. Not that there was much to see—beyond the bones was an empty, dark room with a single torch to illuminate it.

I spun around, hesitant to touch the bones after the revulsion I'd felt before. Where was I? The last thing I remembered was fighting Sark and the others, and then

Doran grabbing me and pressing something to my face. I'd been unable to stop him, and then I'd woken up here. Whatever he'd done must have knocked me unconscious for some time...which meant I was being held by the Dragons.

I reached out for my bond with my mates, but felt nothing from them. Something was blocking me, like a wall I couldn't find my way around. I had no way to tell if they were injured or even still alive. And worst of all, without the bond they'd never be able to find me.

Could it be the bones preventing me from reaching them? I hesitantly wrapped a hand around one of them, part of an arm from the looks of it, and felt that same horror and repulsion as before. I quickly let go and gasped, stepping back, except there was no escape from the cage that surrounded me.

Footsteps approached from across the room and I tensed. A woman with long, luxurious red hair moved toward the bone cage with confident, deliberate steps. She wasn't particularly tall, but she practically glowed with strength and power, and even though her skin was unwrinkled, her green eyes held the wisdom of more years than one person should ever live through. She was so beautiful it was hard to look away from her, even though I sensed a darkness within her I'd never felt before...except from the shades.

There was no doubt in my mind who this was—Nysa, the Black Dragon.

My mother.

She stopped in front of the cage and I fought the instinct

to shrink back from her. The way she looked at me made my skin crawl, but I wouldn't cower in her presence. I was the next Black Dragon, and I would stand tall and face her, even if it was the hardest thing I'd done before.

She gave me a smile that was so lovely it made my chest hurt. "I've been looking for you for a long time, Kira." She reached for me through the cage, as if to stroke my hair. "You're more beautiful than I ever imagined."

I flinched back, my heart pounding. "Stay away from me."

Her hand fell and her smile vanished. "I'm sorry. You must think me a monster, don't you?"

I didn't answer, trying to gain control of my emotions. This woman was my enemy, and I was meant to destroy her and take her place, but she was also my mother. Some primal part of me longed to hear those kind words from her and wanted to lean into her touch. Yet I couldn't forget all the horrible things done in her name, or the misery she'd inflicted upon the world for hundreds of years.

She let out a soft sigh. "Yes, in some ways I am a monster, but there's a reason for everything I have done, and there's much you don't know." She paused and regarded me with those ancient eyes. "You see, sometimes you must become a monster to protect the world from something even worse."

I had no idea what she was talking about, and wasn't sure I could believe anything she said anyway. But she'd kept me alive for some reason, and that meant something.

"What do you want with me?" I asked.

"Right now, I only want you to rest." She gripped the bone cage in front of me and gazed into my eyes. "As much as it saddens me, your fight will soon be over."

With those words she turned and walked away, leaving me to wonder what she had in store for me. I desperately reached for my mates again through our bond, but couldn't find them. I was truly on my own here.

But I wouldn't give up. I would fight back. I would find a way to escape. I would be reunited with my mates again.

And then we would stop the Black Dragon and her men, once and for all.

ABOUT THE AUTHOR

New York Times Bestselling Author Elizabeth Briggs writes unputdownable romance across genres with bold heroines and fearless heroes. She graduated from UCLA with a degree in Sociology and has worked for an international law firm, mentored teens in writing, and volunteered with dog rescue groups. Now she's a full-time geek who lives in Los Angeles with her husband and a pack of fluffy dogs.

Visit Elizabeth's website: www.elizabethbriggs.net

ALSO BY ELIZABETH BRIGGS

Standalones:

Hollywood Roommates

The Chasing The Dream Series:

More Than Exes (#0.5)

More Than Music (#1)

More Than Comics (#2)

More Than Fashion (#3)

More Than Once (#4)

More Than Distance (#5)

The Future Shock Trilogy

Future Shock

Future Threat

Future Lost

Made in the USA
Monee, IL
09 November 2021

81743170R00121